The Map of Azoons

The Map of Azoons

E. B. Anderson

RESOURCE *Publications* · Eugene, Oregon

THE MAP OF AZOONS

Resource Publications
An Imprint of Wipf and Stock Publishers
199 W. 8th Ave., Suite 3
Eugene, OR 97401

www.wipfandstock.com

PAPERBACK ISBN: 978-1-6667-1718-1
HARDCOVER ISBN: 978-1-6667-1719-8
EBOOK ISBN: 978-1-6667-1720-4

SEPTEMBER 10, 2021

To Mark, Katya, Andrew, Maryana,
Aaron, Dennis, and Pat.

Contents

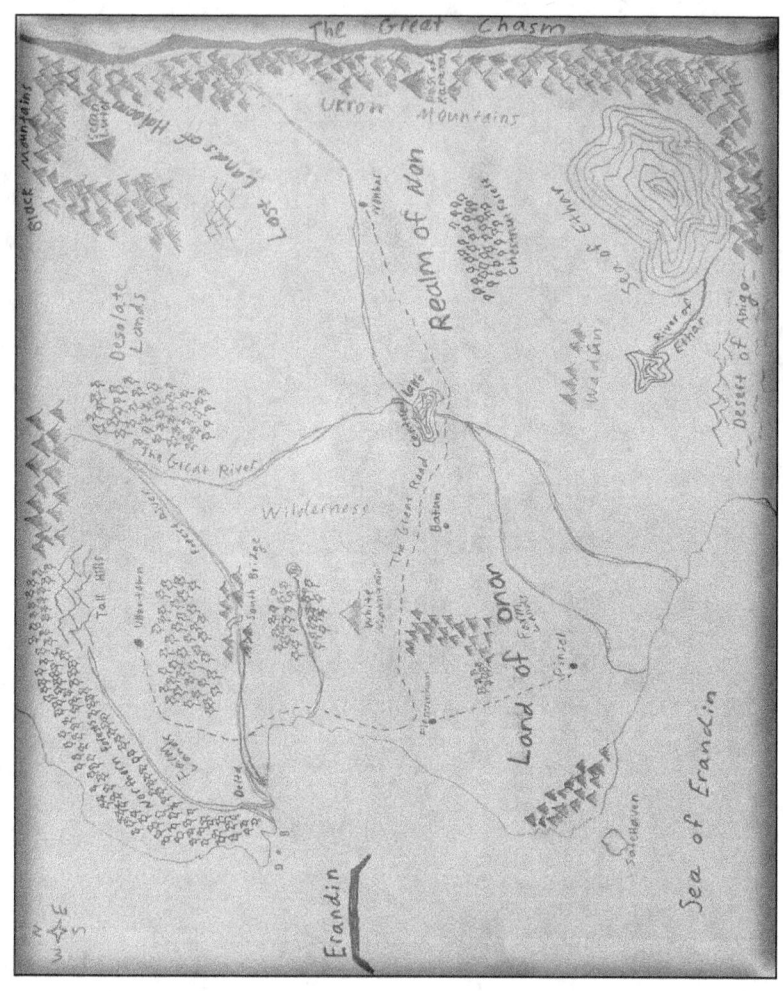

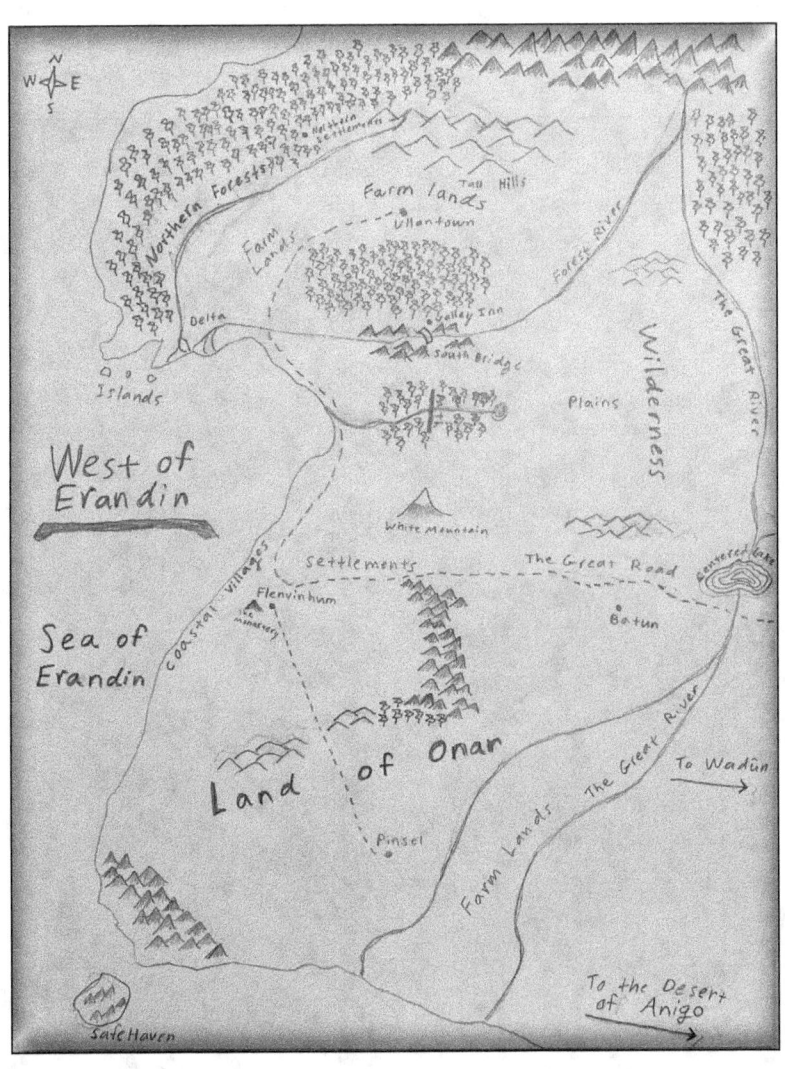

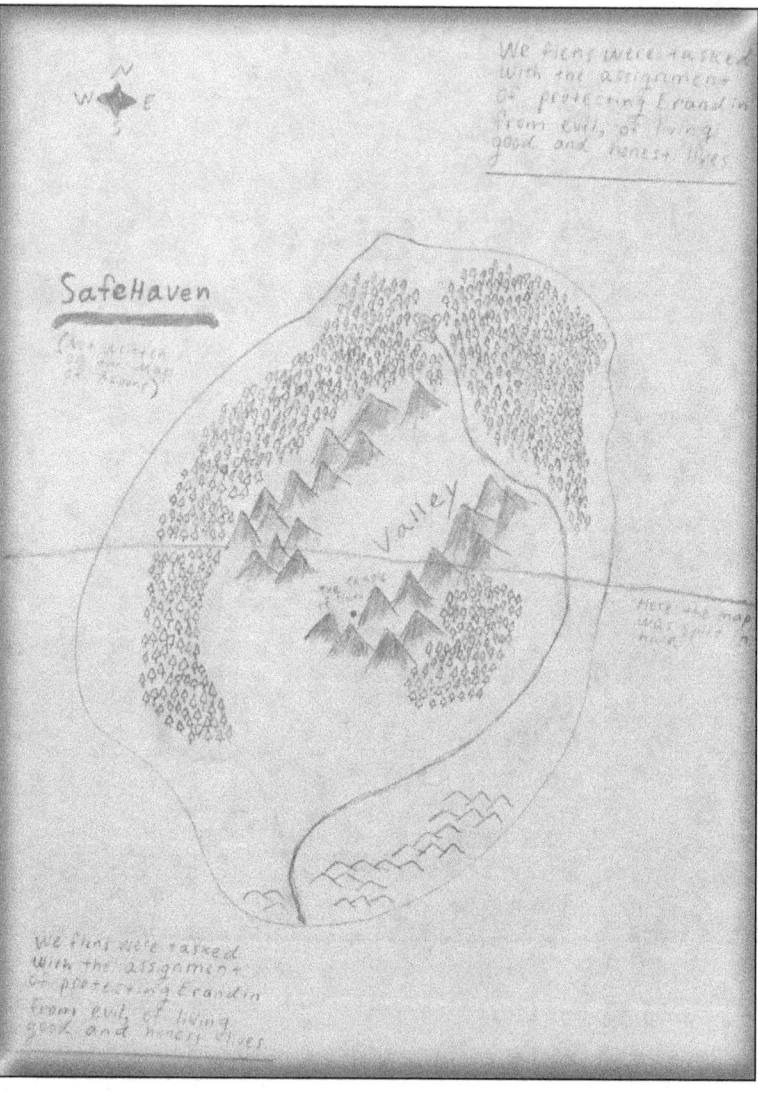

SafeHaven

We fiens were tasked
with the assignment
of protecting Erandin
from evil, of living
good and honest lives.

We fiens were tasked
with the assignment
of protecting Erandin
from evil of living
good and honest lives.

Chapter 1

Life in Ullantown

T HE NIGHT WIND STILLED as the sun broke the horizon, shining down on Ullantown, a large town with farmlands surrounding it from all sides.

Ullantown was really in the middle of nowhere. Beyond the farms and fields were barren lands where few things could survive and where you could expect no help from anyone. Farther north of that were the Northern Forests, which were dark and dangerous and generally unexplored. And if you went far enough south of Ullantown, then you would run into another deep forest, and if you tried to go around it, especially if you went east, then you would eventually enter the Wilderness, which is really a good place to avoid.

As may be guessed, Ullantown was in a dangerous part of Erandin, the great land where the events of this story unfold. But Ullantown itself was rather a friendly and happy place. It was mostly made up of houses, but there were also several small factories and a small university in the middle (if you could call it a university, for it was undeveloped but was all that the people of Ullantown had). So the people who lived there provided for themselves all that they needed, and had very little contact with the outside world.

Now, on that particular morning, one ray of sunlight shone through the window of a small cabin a bit beyond the town limits, shining on the face of a boy flen.

The flen stirred, turning in his bed and pulling the covers over his head.

If it had been up to Nigeb Fortrute, he would have slept in until noon, but the sun rose early on this warm summer day, and he had places to be.

He sluggishly got out of bed, running a hand through his black hair.

Nigeb was a flen. What is a flen? Some explanation of this is necessary, because flens can only be found in Erandin, and the reader has likely never heard of them.

Flens are a nation of people who live in the western part of Erandin. Flens are different from men, and they are not human. They are taller and have fairer faces, generally without beards. They are very skilled in running, being able to run far faster and farther than any man can. And they have fought the evil in Erandin more than any other nation has, and their history reflects it.

It would be easy to mistake a flen for a man, especially if you weren't looking for one. But in those lands and in that time, when the flens were still a large and powerful nation, it was generally well-known who was a flen and who wasn't. Flens do not particularly enjoy being mistaken for men either, and do not easily mix with them.

Nigeb himself was a tall and lean sixteen-year-old who had been living by himself ever since he had turned fifteen, which was when he had moved out from his adoptive family.

He had been living with that family ever since his parents had passed away. To tell the truth, no one knew exactly what had happened to them. But they were gone, and no one had seen them since.

Nigeb had been very young when his parents passed away, and he didn't remember them well, but it was still hard for him. He mourned them on certain occasions every year. He also dearly treasured anything that he had from them, which he kept in his closet.

His adoptive family were not flens, but they owned a farm outside the town limits. For a long time they had hired people to work there. But Nigeb had loved the place: he loved animals and the wilderness with a passion, and this place was the farthest away from town that he could get, so he could spend countless hours tracking deer and wolves without running into anybody.

So as soon as he was old enough, he had volunteered to live there.

His family, however, made sure that he wasn't too lonely. Earl, the oldest sibling in the family, would often stop by the farm and even spend the night. And, of course, his family made sure that he visited them at least twice a week, for hours at a time.

But no matter how interesting and unusual his life of living by himself and spending time in the untamed wilderness seemed to be, Nigeb always felt that something was missing, that his life always followed the same pattern. Something wasn't in place, something very important. He wasn't sure what it was, but he was going to find out.

Sometimes he just felt that something was going to happen, some sort of change of events that he couldn't quite lay his finger on.

And it all started so coincidently, really.

Nigeb had a little arrangement with one of the factories in town that produced dairy products. Because he raised dairy cows, he tended to have a lot of leftover milk. Selling the milk to the factory gave him the chance to make a little money and get rid of all the extra milk.

So when he woke up that morning, he knew he'd spend a good deal of it transporting milk.

He would pour the milk into quart-sized bottles and then put them into four-bottle-sized packages. He would then load all of it into a cart and take it to town.

After he had gotten back from his second trip to town that morning, he realized that he had left two packages of milk behind his dresser.

Well, there was no point in keeping those packages, because he already had too much stored away.

So that meant going back to town.

The town was about a mile away, but he decided to walk there instead of taking the cart, since he only had two gallons of milk. He practically jogged the whole way, knowing that the noon sun would soon start beating down on him.

Once he got to town, he slowed down, staying in the shadows of the houses. He rounded a corner and the large shape of a house blocked out the sun, casting a huge shadow on the ground. It felt so good to be in the shade, Nigeb was almost sorry he had to continue.

As he passed the large house, he noted that it was the one that belonged to Thon and Firm, two cousins, about his age, who lived together and probably owned the largest house in Ullantown. They were also flens, something unusual to see as far north as Ullantown.

As he passed their house, he noticed the two cousins standing on their porch with another, older man.

When Nigeb saw him, he immediately stopped walking and gazed on in amazement.

The stranger was an old man, with a long, white, flowing beard. Dressed in ordinary grayish clothes with a gray cloak, a hood, and a staff gripped in his hands, he had kind of an outstanding face that was very easy to remember and recognize.

The way that he was dressed and the way that he looked and talked all made it obvious that he came from far away. This itself was very unusual. Ullantown was so secluded that people came there only for important business, and what business could there possibly be in a town as small as this one?

Nigeb was about to continue on his way, but taking a second look at the old man made him stay.

You see, spending countless hours in the wilderness does something to a person, and during his last couple years of tracking animals, Nigeb had learned to look for and notice details.

And that's what he couldn't help but notice on the elder man. At first glance, he appeared to be old, far past his prime years, but after Nigeb took a second look, he started to notice evidence that said something else.

Good posture, a tall back. A confident grip on the staff. Stable footing, a good balance.

The elder seemed to be in great condition, perfectly capable of doing things that most younger people can do.

Nigeb was greatly puzzled by this, as he felt that the elder was unusually old, in the sense that he knew and had seen many things, but that at the same time there was some superhuman power behind him.

As Nigeb pondered this, he realized the awkwardness that he must have been displaying as he stood there, holding the packages of milk. He would have described himself as "spying on people."

He quickly hurried on, thinking about how bad it was going to feel once he was in the sun again.

However, it seemed like the heat might be a little more tolerable: an eastern breeze shot out from nowhere, stirring the heavy, dense summer air, and ruffling Nigeb's hair.

It felt so great! He stopped for a second to enjoy the refreshment of a little wind.

The breeze shifted in the air, and as it did so, Nigeb's ears caught the conversation on the porch—

—"We flens were tasked with the assignment of serving good and protecting Erandin from evil, of living good and honest lives."

When Nigeb heard that, he stopped dead in his tracks, dropping the bottles of milk, which promptly shattered.

"Forget the milk." he murmured, although when he looked down at the puddles of milk, now seeping away through cracks and holes in the ground, he kind of felt like cursing himself.

But when he thought about what had just been said during the conversation, he entirely forgot about the milk.

What had that man said? Something about flens and protecting *Erandin*? Nigeb was sure he had heard of that somewhere.

And then suddenly it came to him: it was written somewhere in his father's notes!

Nigeb thought back to when he last went through his father's writings. His father must have been a historian or an archeologist, because he had tons of notes and maps on all sorts of different things that had been given to Nigeb as his heritage. But getting down to the point, he definitely remembered reading *"We flens were tasked with the assignment of serving good and protecting Erandin from evil, of living good and honest lives"* somewhere in his father's notes.

So then, how had this complete stranger, whom he had never seen before, been able to quote something from his father's writings, word by word? And he would have had to be reciting it, not making it up on his own, because that was just too impossible

That meant that he had either read it or heard it from somewhere, but Nigeb knew his father's writings had not been published.

The conversation behind him stilled, and Nigeb turned around. But the old man and the cousins weren't on the porch anymore. In fact, they weren't anywhere.

Nigeb considered knocking on the door (he assumed that they had gone inside) and asking the old man how he knew about something that his father wrote, but he changed his mind. He decided that it would be too awkward. Someone more outgoing might have done it but Nigeb wasn't of that type.

Instead, he decided to go look through his father's belongings to see if he could find any information on his father's notes being published, although he doubted it.

Forgetting to clean up the mess of milk he had made, he headed back to his cabin, not even caring about the burning midday sun.

When he got back home, he started digging around in his closet, making a large mess and going through all his father's old belongings, especially the papers and notes, until he found something that caught his eye.

Most of his father's papers were diaries and maps, but what Nigeb grabbed was a scroll that looked like it was from some fairy tale.

When Nigeb had learned to read, he had personally gone through all his father's papers, and this scroll was the one that interested him the most.

He slowly unrolled it.

It was a map, with words and drawings that he did not understand. The map itself was also unusual, with mountains and rivers and forests that Nigeb didn't recognize. In fact, the whole map seemed off charts. But especially intriguing were the words *We flens were tasked with the assignment of serving good and protecting Erandin from evil, of living good and honest lives* written on the top right corner.

A stranger had said word for word what was written on his father's map, and Nigeb himself was starting to have doubts that the map was unimportant.

But if that was so, then it could only mean one thing.

Someone else knew about the map, and about his parents.

Chapter 2

The Encounter

THON AND FIRM LIVED in a quite comfortable house made of the finest material. It was the nicest house on the block, with a large, open front porch and an overhanging balcony. The house was painted a warm olive color and had large open windows that flooded the house with sunlight.

Thon and Firm were quite fond of it and liked to talk about it. They usually tried not to get carried away bragging, but it didn't always work.

They were still young flens at the age of sixteen, living many miles away from their families, who had sent them there to study at the small university Ullantown had to offer.

At least they were cousins, providing each other company.

Thon wasn't exactly serious about his academic career. He was one of those handy, self-taught people who preferred to do things his own way. He was a great carpenter and was always busy in his shed making furniture and wooden souvenirs and tools instead of doing his school assignments. He had a good business going on and pretty much had his career figured out. But though he was a good carpenter, he was a bad flen to live with. Often he didn't care about certain important things, and he was very forgetful, especially when it was his turn to cook supper or wash the dishes.

Firm, on the other hand, was much more organized and intentional in what he did, and was often bothered by his cousin's behavior. He liked getting a proper education and was always trying to be a good student. By nature he was a quiet, unassuming flen, but could handle important things.

However, the event that is about to take place happened during the summer, when the university let out, and when Thon closed up his shop.

***

Our two cousins were actually just getting back from visiting their parents, who lived farther south. Firm was in good spirits, but Thon wasn't thrilled.

"Mom and dad are making me finish my education!" he lamented. "That's three more years of sitting my bottom down in that dusty little classroom! And when mom hears about how badly I'm doing, she's certain to make me retake my classes! I'm doomed to spend the rest of my days in this pathetic little town that nobody knows about! Tell me, how am I supposed to achieve anything when I'm in a town with only one carpenter shop?"

"Hey, that's a good thing," Firm said, "because the closest carpenter is thirty miles away, so people don't really have a choice but to go to you."

"Are you listening to me?" Thon answered. "How am I supposed to become famous if the only person to compete against is myself?"

"Compete only against yourself." Firm remembered the saying. "Plus, it can't be that hard to 'finish your education' when you skip half the assignments."

"My cousin, I am a genius in the making. I can't waste my time buried in a schoolbook." Thon replied.

Firm opened his mouth, planning on saying something witty, but right when it seemed that the cousins would get into a fight, there was a knock at the door.

It very much sounded like someone was using a *stick* to knock on their good, polished, painted, expensive door. And no doubt they were scratching it and tearing up the paint that had been applied just two weeks ago.

Thon nearly levitated off his chair in his rush to answer the door.

"A customer?" he said under his breath, as his hand closed around the door handle. "Can't be that poor excuse of a mailman."

The handle turned and Thon pulled the door back.

It was not the mailman, nor a customer, probably.

It was an old man, with a long white beard, plain clothes and cloak, kind, wise eyes that told his personality, a small smile, and a *staff,* which he must have used to knock on the door, an old-people thing, no doubt.

Thon stood in the doorway for a long moment, taking the scene in.

The old man made no move. Thon frowned at him and then asked. "What do you want, sir? If you're looking for a carpenter, then let me tell you that I'm closed."

"A carpenter?" said the old man, smiling a little. His voice was keen and had a strange ring to it that Thon couldn't quite place. And as every word was said, the young flen could almost hear it echoing inside his head. "Yes, I am looking for a carpenter, but the business that I bring is bad and will give you little profit. I have come here for you, and for your cousin back there."

"Me?" asked Firm, astounded. He was now standing in the doorway. "You came here for me?"

"And me." Thon said grumpily. He didn't feel like being left out.

The old man continued. "I have traveled over vast distances in my search for a certain number of flens, scattered across Erandin as they were, but who have always been meant to come together. And my travels have brought me here, in search of you two, Thon and Firm Arolin."

Thon started at that. "You know our names?"

"Yes, I know your names."

Thon was suddenly aware of the fact that the old man still hadn't told them what he was doing at their house. He just kept telling them things that only seemed to make sense to someone who was old, and *wise*.

Thon's first thought was to be suspicious but then he realized that he and Firm had never asked him why he was there in the first place.

"Sir," Thon said quietly. "You say that you are here for us, yet I very much fail to see why." He raised his eyebrow after he said this.

"You want to know why I'm here?" the old man replied, as his eyes flashed. "I don't suppose you are familiar with the terms 'We flens were tasked with the assignment of serving good and protecting Erandin from evil, of living good and honest lives'?"

"No." Thon said flatly and evenly.

"But we are flens." Firm added.

The old man shook his head a little. "Where do I start? O well, why don't we go for a walk? It'll be good to stretch our legs and breathe some fresh air. I will explain everything along the way."

He took to the road, his cloak swirling in the breeze.

Thon would have offered to do something else, but he somehow knew that the old man was set on what he was doing, and he could either follow him or stay behind. He also realized that there was something inside of him that pulled him to the old man, something very persistent.

Firm was already on his way down the steps, so why not tag along?

"It'll be quick," he told himself. "At least, oh, at least I hope."

He bounded down the steps and hurried after his cousin.

The old man was going at a fast pace, especially for someone so old. Firm was practically jogging to keep up with him, so Thon really had to put some effort into catching up with them.

The old man seemed to look over as Thon caught up, and then he began speaking.

"Flens are a very noble nation, full of excitement and unusualness, and I have long been fond of your folk. I have had many dealings with flens, and it is for this that I come to you now.

"You see, flens have been greatly involved in fighting the evil of Erandin, especially the Hondaloom, who is the greatest enemy of all."

"The Hondaloom, the source of all evil." Firm whispered.

Thon looked sidelong at his cousin. He did not wish to hear that name of evil.

The old man waited, then spoke.

"My task has also been to fight him, and so I have worked much with the flens, especially the flens of Old, the mighty warriors who carried the title of Azoons, and who fought the Hondaloom from the beginning of Erandin's time."

"The flens of Old?" Thon asked in astonishment. "Why, they lived many generations of men ago! Hundreds and hundreds of years have passed since their time."

Then a flicker of doubt, or perhaps amazement, shone in his eyes, and he asked. "Sir, how old are you?"

A smile tugged at the corners of the old man's mouth, and he answered. "Know that I was in the Beginning of Time, and that I have seen many things, but that does not concern us right now."

Thon almost said something; he could feel the words forming on his tongue, but he held back at the last moment.

The old man looked down the empty streets, something unusual to see in Ullantown, and then continued. "The flens have done much in the fight against the Hondaloom, and have displayed great amounts of courage and heroism. But all the deeds of the past have not been enough to defeat this evil. The Hondaloom has been quiet for many years, and both flens and men alike have let down their guard. But he is becoming more active than ever. His power and his rule is growing, and already some lands have become subject to him. He is the self-proclaimed king of Erandin.

"But the things and deeds of the past were only setting the stage. The deciding battle, the *final* battle, between good and evil is still to come."

"And you're saying that this is true?" Firm asked, innocently.

"I gave you this narration in a very simple and reduced way, but yes, it is true." the old man replied in his powerful, steady voice.

"So then, if this is supposedly true," Thon began slowly, "who's gonna fight the final battle between good and evil?"

The old man's face steadily became very serious.

"You will help."

Chapter 3

The Gathering of Flens

HE LETTER ARRIVED THE next day.

It was strange, unexplainable, and, above all, even more unusual than the conversation Nigeb had heard the previous day.

He was still pondering on the meaning of the map and what it had to do with everything when the letter came.

It wasn't delivered by anyone, at least as far as Nigeb knew. It sat on his desk, next to his bed. How it made its way there Nigeb could not imagine. But after searching his house and finding no possible way in except by the bolted door, he began to feel very frightened.

Between the letter and how it could have possibly arrived, it's understandable that Nigeb spent some time dumbstruck.

Slowly, he repeated the letter out loud to make sure he had read everything correctly.

It read as follows:

> *Dear Nigeb Fortrute,*
>
> *You, as the son of the noble Nilleb and Rosalyn Fortrute, have been chosen and invited to go on a journey and to become a part of Dominum's Kingdom.*
> *You must be ready. Do not stall.*

*Go to the big oak tree outside of the town's university,
at precisely twelve o'clock on Friday, the second day of June,
where you will receive further instructions.*
   *I know that you seek information about your parents. I
will give it to you if you will meet me, for they were friends
of mine.*
                              Dominum's son

Nigeb's heart nearly stopped every time he read the name
Dominum. He had heard incredible accounts of Dominum, and
yet he understood so little that the name was like that of a stranger
to him. And he didn't know Dominum to have a son, which made
him skeptical.

He had felt a tremendous amount of longing at the thought
of learning about his parents, but the mention of a journey and
sharing in a kingdom troubled him.

Nigeb questioned the validity of the letter. He couldn't understand how anyone knew about his parents, and why he was so
important to Dominum's son.

He felt a strong urge to rip the letter apart, to forget about
its contents, which were causing him so much uncertainty and
trouble. He wanted to throw it away and say that it was a lie. But
as he read the letter for the hundredth time, the letters and words
seemed to penetrate him and blaze through his mind in a messy
stream of inky rivers so that he could not put it down.

Not being able to read anything anymore, he attempted to
crumple the letter. He felt his muscles contract, he could feel his
fingers squeezing, but he couldn't curve them or harm the letter
in any way.

Finally, he dropped down on his bed.

"What am I thinking?" he asked himself.

This letter could possibly be the start of a new beginning, a
long hoped for change. There was nothing Nigeb wanted more in
the world than to learn about his parents.

He decided to follow the letter's instructions, no matter what it would lead to, because he knew he would never forgive himself if he didn't.

He looked at the letter, still in his hand, and read it one more time.

It was Friday, the second day of June, the date on which he was to go to the university.

He put on his cloak, took the letter, and stepped out of the door.

***

Carefully approaching the far side of the university's grounds, Nigeb scanned the horizon, looking for a particularly large oak tree.

His experience of being aware of his surroundings didn't fail him now, and he almost immediately spotted the large tree, covered in old, cracked bark, and towering over even the roof of the distant university.

In the shade of the tree's vast branches sat a number of figures, but due to their distance, Nigeb couldn't say how many.

There was obviously some truth to what the letter said, but uneasiness can have some truth to it as well. This is why Nigeb felt more comfortable approaching the group from the farther side of the oak, ensuring that he would see them before they saw him.

He quietly crept over to that side of the tree. This is where he hesitated for a moment, unsure of whether he should just walk in or wait. Not hearing any conversation, he decided it was a good moment to make his appearance.

Standing up to his full height, he briskly walked around the tree, over to where the figures where resting, and promptly pretended not to notice their shocked expressions.

"Wow, he just appeared out of nowhere." one of them said, clearly surprised, and quickly getting up from his reclined position.

It took Nigeb a second to realize that it was Thon. Firm was seated on the grass next to him, clearly as surprised as his cousin. Nigeb nodded to them in the typical Ullantown greeting fashion:

he wasn't sure if they knew him but he definitely knew who they were.

Due to the blank expressions on the cousins' faces, Nigeb realized that they had no idea who he was and quickly turned to take in the others.

The first thing that struck him about this group was that most of them weren't even over twenty. They were all Nigeb's age, about sixteen through twenty. They all seemed mature, capable of acting like adults, and were all fit and able. Several of them had charming faces, and most didn't look like they were from around Ullantown. And they were all flens.

One was clearly older than the rest. He was the only one of the group who seemed to be in his early twenties, had long, brown hair, and easily stuck out in the group as the oldest and the most experienced.

Now, everything just described happened in a second, not really giving anyone a chance to react as Nigeb promptly pulled out the letter and put it up to the face of the nearest person, who happened to be the older one, described earlier.

Not very polite of Nigeb, considering that he didn't even introduce himself, but he was much too exasperated to notice or stop himself. He was still lacking in this skill.

"Can you explain this?" he inquired.

The older flen looked up at Nigeb, and then slowly reached out for the paper.

He then scanned it with lightning speed. In fact, all Nigeb saw was his eyes dart from the top of the page right to the bottom of it. It was all so fast, Nigeb doubted that he had actually read it.

"Yes, he's the one," the flen said.

The flen next to him leaned over and read the paper himself.

"Are you sure this is him, Levi?" the flen asked. "Seems strange that Dominum's son personally called us seven, but then only gave a letter to this one. It is clear that he hasn't met him. When Dominum's son talked to you, he said that he was very particular about the eight flens he had picked. Surely he would have personally met this one as oppose to giving him a letter. Hard to know who this letter actually came from, and forces of evil are hard at work."

"Dominum works in many mysterious ways, and I suppose his son does as well. Everyone is called in a unique way." the older flen, Levi, answered. "I wouldn't be so quick to doubt, Oser."

Nigeb would have interjected by then, but he was completely speechless at being thought of as a phony and then being referred to as a *force of evil*. Worse yet was being ignored by total strangers, who were talking about him at that very moment like he wasn't there. He gestured wildly with his arms and tried to say something, but at that moment Levi and Oser finally acknowledged his presence. Levi spoke before he had a chance to.

"I apologize, but I do believe that you've neglected to introduce yourself, although I do think your name is Nigel, if the letter is true. My own name is Levi."

The flen had mispronounced Nigeb's name, and it was all he could do not to scream in frustration. But he then recollected himself. "I guess I have neglected to introduce myself. The name's Nigeb. *Nee-g-eb.* N as in *nest.* I as in *piano.* G as in *get.* E also as in *get.* B as in any B."

"Ah, I see that I have misread the name." Levi said, glancing at the letter, still in his hand. "I am happy to see that you have joined us and decided to go with us to Flenvinhum, the great capital city of the flens."

"Flenvinhum?" Nigeb stuttered. "Dear me, correct me if I'm wrong, but did you say I'm going to Flenvinhum? I will do no such thing! I belong in Ullantown, and besides, who the heck are you guys?"

"Why don't you sit down, Nigeb?" Levi asked. "It is quite a nice day, and the grass is fresh and soft. Then I will try my best to explain all this."

After Nigeb had (reluctantly) sat down and made himself comfortable, Levi continued.

"As you know, I'm Levi. This one's Oser." He pointed to Oser.

"Call him Athor." That was directed to a blonde-haired, young flen who also happened to be the tallest and most muscular of the group.

"That's Thon. Firm, his cousin, is seated next to him. The one on the far side of the tree is Kevin. And the one eating tomorrow's dinner is Tenzin."

That won a smile from Tenzin, who, indeed, was going through the luggage (of which there was plenty).

Levi looked back at Nigeb, interlaced his fingers, and then leaned back. "Now, what is it that you seek to know?"

"I wish to know about my parents." Nigeb answered.

Levi shrugged his shoulders. "I am afraid I cannot help you. I've never heard of them."

Nigeb looked around. "Are you implying that not one of you is Dominum's son?"

Levi replied with a bit of agitation, the type that comes with dealing with one who knows far less than yourself. "Do I look like Dominum's son to you?"

"I wouldn't know," Nigeb answered. "I've never heard of him."

A silence followed this.

Then Levi looked very fervently into Nigeb's eyes, and the latter flen experienced the presence of a fiery heart. "How is it that the news of Dominum's son never reached you? He is the son of him who created Erandin into its existence. He's the son of the real King of Erandin! He has come from Dominum's own land to end the false reign of the Hondaloom!"

"But with all due respect," Nigeb said, although he was holding back from saying "*like I care,*" "that is really not what I have come for. I assume that you could alert Dominum's son about the fact that I want information about my parents and that I absolutely refuse to go to Flenvinhum. Besides, traveling to Flenvinhum over the land that separates us from it is dangerous."

"The only way that you could learn more about your parents would be to meet Dominum's son, and the only way that you could meet him would be to go to Flenvinhum. There is no other way," Levi answered.

Nigeb seethed. "This Dominum's son seems like a far-fetched theory to me. Are you quite sure about all this?"

Levi answered. "There is a prophecy that speaks of the rise of eight flens, brought together against the Hondaloom, and of the doom of evil. Nigeb, you seem as though you greatly seek to know more about your parents. But Dominum's son will offer more than just that. The tides of change are at hand. Dominum's son seeks to defeat the evil Hondaloom. On which side shall you be on?"

"But why should I go?" Nigeb challenged. He was still skeptical, but he felt his indecision waver a bit. He counted the flens present there, including himself, and found that there were eight of them. "I know not of this Dominum's son, and I certainly do not wish to travel to Flenvinhum."

Levi answered. "I tell you this: Dominum's son has personally invited you and offered to share treasured (I believe) information. Of events that may happen in the future I do not know much of but I assume they will be dangerous and hard. However, I promise you the friendship and loyalty of this company and myself, and that you will share in whatever rewards we may have."

Nigeb answered. "I don't need your loyalty at the moment, thank you very much. But I do want to know more about my parents, though I feel this is all a little forced. I assume you will like to hear that I'm intrigued; I'd like to learn more. I will go see this son-of-Dominum, but I make no promises."

"Excellent." Levi said, motioning for everyone to get up. "I knew you were a nice chap. Now if you don't mind running home for your most valued possessions only, we shall meet at the gates of Ullantown in precisely an hour. That leaves you the trip to your house plus the trip back and only a small time of packing. Hurry up now."

"One more thing," Nigeb said, grabbing his letter. "You keep using the words Dominum's son, which I doubt is his real name. And if it's not Dominum either, then what is it?"

"That," Levi said, laughing, "is another reason you should go to Flenvinhum, as you should find it out for yourself."

Chapter 4

The Valley Inn

NIGEB RACED THROUGH ULLANTOWN, passing many people, even those on horseback. He went out the gates, over several hills, and to his front door. He quickly found a travel bag and packed it with a change of clothes, a cloak, and some essential belongings. He also packed the letter from Dominum's son and his father's map, which for some reason he felt would be important.

After this, he quickly wrote a letter to his adoptive parents, telling them that he was going on a journey, and that they shouldn't worry about him. He couldn't explain in details why he was going, he just knew that he was.

He ran back to Ullantown, stopped by the post office to drop off the letter, and then went back to the gates, where he found the flens.

They had already been to the stables and had brought back eight strong horses.

When Levi saw him approaching, he called out, "Hurry up now, there's a good chap. We are ready to leave and plan to be well beyond the town by nightfall. Saddle up."

***

"My face!" Tenzin complained, after being hit by a thin branch.

"Ouch . . . ouch . . . " Firm was mumbling over and over again, as he moved uncomfortably on his saddle.

"Did I just swallow a bug?" Thon said after a loud gulp, his face horrified.

The flens had reached the forest south of Ullantown in a full day's ride. They had been traveling on horseback in the dense forest for three days now, all because Athor was convinced that he knew a shortcut.

The trees in this forest had grown so thickly together that it was nearly impossible to see someone several yards in front of you. The branches were like knives sinking in you from all directions. Some of the flens were starting to doubt that it was possible to navigate in this thicket.

The flens had also gotten separated several times, which was horrifying, because once you got lost, there was little chance to get out.

No one wanted to be the one who got lost again, and some of the flens even took the precaution of linking themselves together with ropes.

Spending several nights in that dreadful forest was just as stressful, because you never knew what was several paces away from you as you slept, and the flens tended to sleep in a tight circle, with the bravest on the outside. That usually included Levi, who seemed to be cold blooded to the point that nothing could scare him, Athor, who was just as much a daredevil as he was muscular, and Oser, whenever he felt brave enough (that usually depended on the weather).

And also Nigeb, because he felt that his experience in the wilderness should be a form of helping and encouraging others. And yes, he still couldn't quite believe that he was going to Flenvinhum.

He spent most of his time at the rear of the group, keeping to himself and staying in the background. Some of the flens, however, were making that hard by constantly bringing him up in their conversations, and then wondering where he was (which, of course, led to finding him and pulling him into the conversation).

Mostly, Nigeb just didn't feel like he fit into this wisecracking group who seemingly already knew each other.

However, he was starting to become more comfortable with them. Which, I guess, is what being in good natured company can do to you.

Which is why, on the fourth day of their journey, Nigeb found himself at the beginning of the line, which was where all the conversation was happening. Understandably, it was mostly between Levi and Athor.

"Remind me never to listen to you again!" Levi was saying through gritted teeth.

"You can say that again!" Athor said, as if he was talking about someone else and not himself.

"You said that 'there is a shortcut, which will save us days'! And yet there is *nothing* that even closely resembles a shortcut in this cursed forest." Levi said, wildly swinging his arms.

"I could have sworn that someone told me about a shortcut!" Athor said, peering into the trees. "Maybe we entered at the wrong place?"

"Yes, maybe, but there is one problem," Levi said smoothly. Then he yelled. "If you told me once, then you told me a million times that you were confident we had entered at the right place!"

Athor wasn't paying much attention, however. Instead, he was staring out into the trees.

"We've got to be close, I can feel it," he was murmuring.

Seeing that he couldn't get Athor's attention, Levi turned to Nigeb.

"What's your opinion on where we are?" he asked.

To tell the truth, Nigeb was quite startled. He had gotten so interested in the conversation that he hadn't realized how closely he was riding to Levi and Athor. He quickly realized that he also had no idea where they were; he had been so wound up in his thoughts lately that he hadn't been paying attention to his surroundings.

So his answer was quick and short.

"I'm not sure."

Levi sighed and looked back.

Nigeb could tell that some of the flens behind him were getting agitated. Nobody wanted to spend any more time in that untamed forest, and the flens were making that known with their quiet protests.

Athor had started to pull away, and everyone was in a hurry to catch up. It was definitely noticeable that the trees were less dense.

Suddenly, the forest opened up to a beautiful prairie, and Nigeb's face was flooded with sunlight.

The flens cheerfully rode out into the spacious field, enjoying the beautiful, open area, and shouting (mostly at Athor, but it was hard to tell whether they were thanking him or criticizing him).

Several flens dismounted their steeds to stretch their legs, but Nigeb urged his horse out into the field. He was not too shabby at horseback riding, but the last couple of days had given him some unique experience, and he wanted to enjoy some riding in an open field.

After making a few rounds, however, Nigeb felt a strong sense of hunger. He then realized how poorly he had eaten the last few days. So he got off next to where the flens were making camp.

Levi and the witty Oser had already started a fire. Athor was talking about hunting game (it was put to a stop as soon as Thon pulled out some sausages). And a few of the flens were sprawled out on the ground.

As the smell of roasted sausage filled his nostrils, Nigeb looked to the south, the direction of the South Bridge. Across the horizon, as far as the naked eye could see, there was a thin but prevailing line of gray. That gray line was the beginning of a long canyon over which the South Bridge was located. It was the same canyon that the celebrated and legendary Don, also known as Don the Wild, had passed over so many centuries ago, as he led an expedition into the untamed north.

Interestingly, the north was still considered untamed (and trust me, Nigeb believed it).

Nigeb shaded his eyes, trying to get a better glimpse of where the South Bridge might be.

"We'll be crossing over that tomorrow, my late-coming friend."

Nigeb looked over and was surprised to see that Levi was standing behind him.

"We will spend the night at an inn and then leave tomorrow morning." Levi continued. "I want to get through the bridge as fast as possible. Who would've thought that the South Bridge could be worse than that forest?"

"Worse how?" Nigeb asked uneasily.

"Just plain dangerous," Levi replied. "I wanted to come out of the forest on the west side, and then travel towards the Great Road. We would then follow the Great Road over the Forest River, which flows at the bottom of the canyon. After that we would follow the coastline to Flenvinhum, which would be far safer than the path we are on. We will now have to cross the South Bridge, go through yet another forest, and possibly pass through mountains, and only then will we come to Flenvinhum, Dominum help us. I am not accustomed to this area, and was counting on Athor, who claimed he knew the way.

"The canyon before us stretches for fifty miles to the west before there is a crossing, which is at the Great Road. You would have to travel even farther east before you could find a way across. Either way, the terrain would be brutal. The South Bridge is our only option."

Levi sighed.

"There isn't time to spend a week battling the northern wilderness as we try to reach the Great Road, and it is far more dangerous to travel along the forest than through it. I have known that luns densely inhabit the area around the South Bridge, but I also heard of a little inn where we could spend the night. The people there are fair and honest and could point us in the right direction. They also know how best to handle luns."

If only there was a thing Levi didn't know about.

Although now he was starting to scare Nigeb a bit, for luns are a very dangerous people that live mostly in the untamed wilderness, especially in the north. Many of them also live in the

Lost Lands of Holoom, and still openly serve under the ranks of the Hondaloom. They are not human. They are all tall and bulky, standing at least a foot over any flen or man. They are vicious and unpleasant in lifestyle, and have ugly faces and deeply tanned skin.

They were the first to side with the Hondaloom, and so lost their place among men and flens. After that, they retreated to the dark and wild places, and became more evil because of it.

They should most certainly be considered the enemy.

"When will we be in their territory? And will we be in danger of them?" Nigeb asked.

Levi laughed. "We've been in their territory ever since we crossed into that forest, and we most certainly are in danger of them, as anyone would be." he said.

"Seriously?" Nigeb hardly managed to say it as he lost his breath.

"Of course," Levi replied. "But I could guarantee you that there wasn't a single lun in that forest. Very few people are known to live there and luns aren't included. We are only in danger of them now."

Levi looked back at the rest of the flens.

"And lucky for us," he said. "I also heard of that inn. Let us have some late lunch before it fully disappears."

Needless to say, Nigeb really enjoyed the meal. After the last scrap was finished and everyone was satisfied, the flens spent a long while discussing various routes, and the possible danger that lay ahead. Then their conversation turned to the wonders of Flenvinhum, and other such things involving it. Finally, their talk turned to history and legend, to the struggle between the evil Hondaloom and his forces and Dominum and his son, aided by the noble and great flens of Old. They discussed battles and stories of daring adventures and times of great danger and heroism. Many of the flens were particularly fond of songs, and after a while Oser got up and said.

"My fiddle is in my bag, shall I get your harp, Athor?"

Tenzin said, "Excuse me," and went to get his own harp.

"Bring mine too," Levi added. "It's the flute in my cloak."

After Oser and Tenzin returned, and everyone was seated, the four flens began all at once. And as they began playing the beautiful, enchanting melody, they began to sing in deep, quiet voices and hum to the rhythm.

This is somewhat how the song went, although there was more to it, so much that I didn't record it all:

The journey's long and tough,
But we know that there's enough
Of love and trust
And go we must.

We must leave our town,
Before he comes down.
Because the Hondaloom
May cause our doom.

And end us all
And we will fall.
But strong we are
And go we far.

Far out of sight,
Out of his might.
To Flenvinhum
We go and come.

The mountains there are tall and dark
And many a traveler has left his mark.
There the country's fair
With music in the air.

The meadows and trees are green,
The waters clear and clean,
The oaken forests are tall,
The beloved Whitened Fall.

Shone down the stars on high,
On the valleys standing by.

There the first flens came through
To see a sky of clear and blue.

So keep on going,
Swimming or flying,
And we shall come
To Flenvinhum!

They sang well into the evening, and only when the sun began to set did they get up and continue.

***

The sun was setting and the flens had traveled to the edge of the canyon. Several of the flens, mostly Athor and Oser, had wanted to go right to the cliffy edge of the canyon and see if they could go down it and up the other side. Most of the flens had heard of how dangerous the South Bridge could be. There were many reasons, but none were in the least good, and everyone was open to the idea of crossing the large canyon some other way.

Levi had completely shut down the idea by reminding them all that there was a bridge for a reason (the fact that there were so few crossings also proved how dangerous it was to make ways across the valley).

Instead, he brought up the subject of a warm dinner, which convinced everyone to head to the inn.

Nigeb personally didn't need to be reminded of dinner: he had spent the last three days thinking nonstop about sitting down at a large table, in a nice, comfortable house, and sharing a meal with his new friends. So far, the only bonding time he had had with them was horseback riding through that cursed forest (may all its trees wither!), and then eating small portions of fire cooked food once a day, while having to crouch on the ground.

Definitely not a proper way to meet new friends.

Although some of the more adventurous flens actually enjoyed camping in the forest, most of them were relieved to finally have a roof over their heads.

The flens saw a sign saying *Valley Inn*, and after that they finally caught sight of the inn itself. It looked like nothing impressive, but the flens were content with the hospitable air it had. The inn was a large house, made of large logs stacked on one another, and completed with a roof and chimney. It was surrounded by a fence, and several lit windows proved that people were around.

After making their way around the fence, the little group of exhausted travelers finally made it to the front gate, only to be confronted by a suspicious guard.

He was greatly surprised to find flens this far north, and asked them many questions, including where they had come from and where they were going.

After doing a quick search through their bags, he explained that, due to the rough citizens that occupied the land, all weapons and arms were forbidden in the inn. He then confiscated their tools, knives, swords, and even Levi's short sword, which he wore out of his land's tradition.

"Take good care of it," Levi said as he handed it over to the guard. "It was my grandfather's, and it is special to my family. Its name is FireCleaver."

"I will," the man answered. "And tomorrow you shall receive your belongings on the way out."

After entering the large front door, the flens signed in for the night, ordered their dinner, and then headed up to their rooms.

Oser was the one who paid for everything, as he was the only flen who had any money, and was pleased about only getting four rooms: one for two flens each.

Nigeb didn't linger long in the small and plain room that he was sharing with Levi. The old beds and mattresses provided weren't much to look at.

So he dumped his travel bag on the bed and got ready to head downstairs.

But as the bag settled on the bed, some of its contents spilled out, including the envelope containing the map from his father.

Nigeb stooped down to retrieve his belongings, and promptly knocked the envelope down the space between the bed frame and the wall. He tried forcing his hand through the crack, but it was nowhere near wide enough.

He frantically searched for a way to retrieve the envelope, but the bed was both too short to crawl under and too heavy to lift without assistance.

Levi had walked out the door a minute before, so when Nigeb attempted to move the bed on his own, all he got were cramped fingers. It was the heaviest bed that he had ever come across.

"What is the deal with these exasperating beds?" he mumbled, greatly annoyed.

Repositioning his travel bag so that it leaned against the wall, Nigeb left the room and headed to the diner, deciding to get the envelope out later with the help of Levi.

The diner was small, dark, and stuffy. Nigeb had a hard time trying not to gag from the debilitating smell of stale cheese.

The dining room was surprisingly packed. Besides our eight flens (who took up a lot of space, I daresay), there were half a dozen rough-looking travelers, and another group of mean-looking thugs.

The thugs sat at the end of the diner, away from the light, and covered in shadows. Nigeb couldn't get a good look at them, but he clearly noticed them watching him out of their dark cloaks.

Nigeb could just make out their dark eyes, shining out of the shadows, as the eyes of cats and dogs do. A stench rose up from their direction, and he felt an iciness emanating from them.

Unable to look away, he stared at them as if it were a staring contest, until, finally, the food arrived.

It was a combination of bread, meat, vegetables, and a little wine. Although it may have seemed plain to some, the food appeared delicious to the flens.

For years to come, Nigeb would consider this meal to be one of his finest ones, as he was surrounded by friends in what seemed the midst of evil.

The meal didn't end very quickly, as all of the flens were pleased to finally have a proper supper, and it was well into the night before Nigeb first got up and headed to his room.

As he started up the stairs, he thought he heard a commotion in the hallways above. There were a few voices that suddenly quieted down, and loud footsteps seemed to be shuffling down the opposite hallway.

Stopping dead in his tracks, Nigeb listened intently. But the sounds were gone.

Fearing the worst, Nigeb sprinted up the stairs, and running down the painting-lined hall, came to his room.

He couldn't believe his eyes.

The door, the oak wood door with carvings carved deep into its very heart, the door which seemed to be the only thing that would hold up to a breeze in the entire inn, had been smashed down, left to hang awkwardly on its bottom hinge. The doorknob was gone entirely and the part of the door where it used to be was broken through completely. Knife marks were lined deep along its edges, and a huge dent hung around the middle.

The room was no better.

The few bags that Levi and Nigeb owned had been ransacked, the contents spilled out on the floor. Everything had been rummaged through and even the covers had been whisked off the beds. The beds were the only things still in place.

Nigeb, feeling that the situation was pathetic, looked one by one into the other three rooms that the flens had rented.

The situation was the same in each one.

Sprinting back down the stairs, the young flen found that the group of thugs was gone, their table empty.

He put two and two together.

"Help! Help!" he said in a frantically loud whisper as soon as he got to the flens' table. "I am afraid there is no easy way to put this, for goodness' sake, but our rooms have been ransacked! And I think I know who did it!"

As you can imagine, the flens were not at all pleased, although they found that nothing was missing, which puzzled them all. The manager and owner of the inn, when informed, was not in the least understanding (especially when he saw the rooms!), and announced that neither the group that ransacked the rooms nor the flens would ever be allowed back. He then transferred the flens to different rooms, and said that their business in the matter was settled.

Levi, however, secretly told Nigeb he had reasons to believe that the ransackers were somehow related to luns. Warning him not to tell the others, so to keep from panic, he went to the front desk to check the potential luns' names, but came back disappointed. He wasn't able to tell from their names whether or not they were luns. If they really were luns, then they must have changed their names.

After all the excitement and potential danger, Nigeb could hardly sleep.

It was a long night indeed.

Chapter 5

The South Bridge

When Nigeb woke up the next morning, he had a terrible headache. His sleep had been uneasy, and he dreamed that he was stuck in a long, winding maze with no visible way out. The maze was engulfed in darkness, so that he could not see what was attacking him, but he felt dark shadows grabbing and pulling him deeper into the darkness. He suddenly saw a blinding light, and the shadows were thrown back into the darkness. A figure dressed entirely in white, with light radiating from every part of its being, took Nigeb by the hand and led him out of the maze in mere seconds. The darkness closed behind them, and the light opened up before them.

Then Nigeb woke up. His first thought was that the dream was true, and he leapt out of bed. But upon remembering where he was, he calmed down and checked the door. It was still intact, thankfully, although Levi, still in bed, was now grumbling about all the racket Nigeb was making.

Nigeb flopped on his bed, and only then did he remember the map! The map which had fallen behind the bed the night before!

He quickly made his way to the room they had the night before, and easily walked through the doorless doorway. He urgently tried to move the bed (something the reader might laugh at, considering the attempts he had made the night before), and after

several unsuccessful attempts and more cramped fingers, he finally remembered Levi.

Finding his way back to their current room and violently shaking the tired flen, Nigeb finally got him to get up and help, although not before Levi had his own turn at shaking him.

Levi didn't understand what was happening but he followed Nigeb nonetheless to the room they had yesterday. Together, they moved the bed. It took several unsuccessful attempts, which, after all, wasn't something new, but with many tugs and grunts they were finally able to shove it away from the wall a little. Nigeb then immediately pulled out his map, and was happy to see it still in one piece.

After moving the bed back, Levi immediately made his way to their room, grumbling and muttering, and Nigeb didn't see him until breakfast.

***

Nigeb spent the rest of the morning pondering on the meaning of his dream and on the meaning of the break-in, and on the meaning of everything that was making its way into his life.

After the rest of the flens roused themselves, they had a long and enjoyable breakfast of pancakes, eggs, bacon, toast, and tea. Nigeb was also delighted to see that Levi was himself again.

During the long rest after breakfast, the flens felt their spirits waver as they heard from the innkeeper of all the trouble that was happening in those lands, especially of the danger that luns presented, and of how hard their crossing over the canyon could be.

Nigeb especially felt lost at words, as he had not known such danger to have ever crossed his life before. He felt worse as he and the rest of the company left the security of the inn, and rode out into the gloomy lands before them.

The lands were gray and barren, with mountains looming on either side. Few plants grew here, and nothing was to be said of fields or forests, although there was a forest behind them now, and one on the other side of the canyon, which they still had to go through.

The path they traveled on was thin and rocky, and their horses stumbled many times. They felt the land a great depression after their cheery breakfast, and Nigeb felt more and more miserable thinking of all the possible dangers they could come across, like luns and wild animals, or getting lost, not to mention the evil Hondaloom, who it seems was very much against them.

Soon the land began to slope down, not very steeply, but down nonetheless. Their path joined up to a mountain pass, even more a rough path than before. Rocky slopes loomed up on both sides, and the hoof falls of their horses rang out in the eerie silence. As they came up to the top of a ridge, a long and great canyon stretched out before them. It ran along deep beneath them, and its sides were too steep to possibly descend down without proper gear and planning. The Forest River flowed through at the bottom of the canyon, and the sounds of rushing water could be faintly heard from down below. The canyon was not very wide, but stretched down the horizon farther than they could see. Their path ended abruptly, and a bridge, constructed entirely of thick rope, hung before them. It was wide enough for three to walk across side by side and had a railing.

But it was the only evident way of crossing the canyon.

When the flens got off of their horses in order to lead them across the bridge, Levi suddenly held up his hand in the signal of attention.

At first, Nigeb couldn't tell what the problem was, or where it was for that matter. But the thought of it all made him very nervous, and he was not at all pleased about crossing a rope bridge.

It took him a few seconds to realize that Levi was motioning to the other side of the bridge. Several dark figures were starting to move across towards them. The bridge swayed gently as the figures hurried forward, and Nigeb could not understand who they possibly were, although he was starting to have some very bad ideas.

Swiftly the figures came over the bridge, and now it was clear that they were big and ugly, with painted faces and strange clothes, and, above all, were armed to the teeth with the most crude and deadly weapons, such as long spears, bent, razor-sharp swords, and huge, deadly bows.

It was too obvious who they were, and even Nigeb (who had little experience with this type of thing, adventuring and all, and who always did say that tracking animals was far more simpler) was little surprised to hear Levi mutter, "Luns!" under his breath.

For luns they were, and they had now reached the side of the bridge where the flens were, and out the biggest lun had stepped. He was dressed in full armor, and had a large, crude sword held in his hand, which only Athor could have had any chance to lift. He had black and brown ink streaked down his cheeks and forehead, and his bared teeth were yellow and missing in some places. He held up his hand for silence, although he couldn't have asked for more, as all the flens were frozen in their positions and the rest of the luns were silent as well.

"We are the guard of this bridge," the lun, whose name was Yar, said in a deep, raspy voice. "No one goes past without our seeing of the matter, and you have been found guilty, O friends of Dominum's son!"

Tension hung in the air as the lun spoke, and Nigeb wondered how Dominum's son could possibly be helping them now.

The lun continued.

"There is a little something in your possessions, something we cannot let pass on this bridge. If you hand it over, we shall let you pass, if not, woe is to you. The object we desire is a map."

Shuffling and footsteps were heard behind the flens, and several of them turned to see half a dozen luns behind them in the narrow pass, grimacing and gnashing their teeth. All were armed.

While the luns behind the flens stood still, the luns ahead of them moved forward. There were about five of them, and another six were moving up the bridge from the other side of the canyon.

All eyes were on Levi, who was at the head of the company. His horse stomped and flared its nostrils, and Levi mounted it and drew his sword, FireCleaver. The rays of sunlight danced on its edges, and it really did look like it cleaved fire.

The flens would not even consider striking a deal with the luns, and although they didn't know what map it was their enemy desired, there was no question of handing it over. Both sides were waiting for a signal.

No one noticed Athor, sitting upon his horse at the end of the line. He drew his own sword, and did the thing all the luns were least expecting.

"Attack!" Athor roared as he kicked the sides of his horse. The horse had already decided that Athor had gone mad and that he was on a suicide mission, but it had been trained well, and had been taught to do whatever its rider ordered (even if it was a suicide mission). It surged onto the bridge, breaking the stillness.

"Hold," Levi was quietly saying to the flens. "On my count, we surge forward—"

But Levi was interrupted when Athor sped past him at the speed of a blur. Levi could only watch in surprise.

All alone, Athor rode past the two front luns, kicking one with such terrific force that he tumbled down, and thrusting his sword at the other, disarming him and forcing him to stumble back.

A feeling of surprise penetrated the air, and both the luns and the flens moved into position.

Another big lun jumped in Athor's path, and immediately regretted it when Athor's sword came crashing down on his helmet so hard he'd remember it for years to come.

The battle spirit that Athor showed in that little action gave the other flens heart and they drew their swords and sprang forward. Some charged the luns at the beginning of the bridge, and the others fought the luns in the narrow pass.

Nigeb stayed in the middle of the flens, along with Firm. He didn't have any weapons, unlike most of the other flens, and was dreadfully afraid. After all, the luns were armed for battle and they were not. Also, the luns were almost twice the size of the flens.

He watched the flens fight off the luns, using their knives and swords, and using their large bags as shields. But the luns were better trained, and had the advantage. They soon regrouped and came back, driving the flens back off the bridge, while the luns in the narrow pass began to close in.

Nigeb became very frightened as he began to see the situation that they were in.

The flens regrouped on their horses, drawing in a tight circle with Levi and Athor on the outside. They were fighting their way up the bridge, and already it swayed madly, like a ship being tossed by a large storm. The ropes creaked and bits of rock and soil tumbled down into the river, far, far below them.

Then the arrows began to fly. Several luns were perched on inclines at the opposite end of the bridge, and for the first time, they put their arrows to use.

The flens, upon Levi's order, threw up their bags as shields against the arrows. But poor shields their bags were, and they did not stand well against the deadly, yard-long arrows that the luns used.

"Forward! On my count!" Levi yelled as he and Athor charged the luns standing farther up the bridge. "It's no use going back. We must go forward. Follow quickly!"

But as Nigeb turned his horse around to follow the rest of the flens, his steed suddenly reared up, and then leapt forward with a kick. Nigeb was violently thrown down, and he rolled over several times before coming to a stop on the bridge.

Loud yells rose from the luns as they charged towards their easy target.

Athor turned his head, and seeing Nigeb on the ground, his horse fleeing farther up the bridge, pulled his own horse around and made for where Nigeb was frantically trying to get up.

The luns reached Nigeb first, but the flen wasn't quite so easy to catch. He rolled away as the first lun swung his sword, got up, and then pivoted away from Yar, as the brute thrust his sword forward.

Nigeb was almost run over by Athor as the flen came charging up the bridge, making it sway madly. Nigeb, caught off balance, then dove straight into several luns who were trying to avoid falling off the bridge. Nigeb got many bruises and bashes during those

few moments, when it seemed that the whole world was swinging madly. But Yar, however, had it worse off. He didn't move out of the way in time, and was promptly run over by Athor's horse.

The next few moments were a blur. Everyone was yelling. Arrows still flew overhead occasionally. Levi nearly chopped off Nigeb's head with FireCleaver, and Athor, now off of his horse, was moving here and there, and stabbing and slashing. Not to mention the luns that were still out to kill them.

Nigeb could see that the rest of the flens had already made it to the other side of the bridge. But they were still engaged with the luns. Nigeb couldn't see how they possibly could get through without all being killed. And killed in the most unfashionable manner, for luns are not good enemies to have.

Nigeb, Levi, and Athor were forced off the bridge, back to where the flens had originally started. Fighting became hard in the narrow passageway, and Nigeb could no longer see the other five flens.

Levi yelled something out, and Nigeb looked down the far end of the passageway to see an older man with a white beard, dressed in a cloak and wielding a staff.

There was a blinding flash, and the luns fell to the ground, and then some of them got up and began blindly running away.

Nigeb himself began blindly running towards the bridge, his hands held out in front. He unexpectedly crashed straight into Yar, who had lost his large sword and was now holding a smaller, more beautiful sword of great design and splendor. Both flen and lun tumbled down the passage, and Yar's sword flew out of his hand, over the cliff, and down to the river below, or at least that is what Nigeb thought.

Nigeb was grabbed suddenly by his collar, and hauled up onto Levi's horse. Yar rolled away as Levi's and Athor's horses galloped up the passage towards the bridge, without a single lun standing in the way. They made it in several seconds, and were flying across it.

Nigeb looked back and saw the luns pursuing them relentlessly, now that they had recovered from the blinding flash, which Nigeb still couldn't quite understand.

But just before the luns reached the bridge, another blinding flash appeared. When it subsided, it was visible to see that the supports on the end of the bridge opposite to where the flens were heading were cleanly cut. Now that end of the bridge was swiftly falling. The two horses on which the flens rode gave one desperate leap and landed safely on the other side.

But with a frightful cry, Nigeb tumbled off the end of the horse he was on, and disappeared below the edges of the canyon. Both he and the end of the bridge fell away towards the cliff face.

Nigeb shrieked in utter panic, but then felt one groping hand clutch on to a rail on the bridge. Holding on for dear life (quite literally), he and the bridge swung down toward the steep cliff of the canyon, and in two seconds' time, he felt his body crashing into the rocky face. Nigeb's hand slipped off the rope rail, and he was flung down. He fell several yards before landing on a little ledge, several feet wide, and a dozen feet long. He had not seen it earlier, and was greatly relieved for being alive.

He rolled over and right onto a sharp object. He frantically got up, and saw that it was the sword that he had seen Yar drop. It had not fallen to the bottom of the canyon, as it appeared, but had landed on the little ledge. How it had landed was a miracle, as there was another ledge just above him, so that he was in a space between two slabs of rock.

It was hard to believe in miracles in that time and day, but it was hard to ignore the things and events that were happening at that same time.

Nigeb picked up the sword, and gazed thrillingly at its beauty and design. He had never personally had a sword, or any weapon at that, and watching Athor and Levi had made him wish he had one. The sword fit him perfectly, and was the right size and shape for him to handle. It is hard to know how Yar had come by a sword like this—a story for another time, perhaps.

After moving the sword from hand to hand and gently waving it back and forth, Nigeb remembered the situation he was in, and suddenly felt much worse. The excitement he had gotten when he found the sword now faded and he walked to and fro, trying to see if there was a way up, or possibly out.

When he found nothing, he really got scared. Obviously, there was no way out, whether by tunnel or cave, and the cliff was smooth, with very little crevices, not to mention the ledge above him that he would have to climb over. He had personally never done any rock climbing or anything of that sort. Also, the bridge, which was still hanging down the face of the cliff, was too far away to reach or jump for. The only thing to do was wait and hope the other flens figured out a way to reach him.

***

Thon could see where Nigeb had landed. It was a cozy, enclosed little ledge some twenty yards down. The ledge was so well hidden in the cliff that Thon easily could have missed it had it not been for the fact that Nigeb was moving around. Every now and then a glimpse could be caught of him. Thon hoped that he was okay, and that he wasn't terrified because of how close death had come to him. It was a real miracle that Nigeb had somehow landed there. The bridge looked almost like a ladder leading down to the river below. It was close to where Nigeb was. Thon wondered if they could use the bridge to help get the young flen up.

Heated discussion was going on behind Thon. The flens were arguing on what to do next. There was obviously no option of leaving their companion behind, but no one knew what to do.

"Makes me wonder why we brought this one along," Athor was grumbling. "We travel this far, fight through a guard of luns even though we were outnumbered at least two to one, get across this cursed bridge of rope, make it to the other side in time for Dominum's son (for it was Dominum's son) to cut the bridge, leaving more than half of the luns behind, then we overpower the rest, chase them away, and only to find that one of us is missing, now halfway down the canyon! Some adventurer he is. Also makes me wonder if Dominum's son fully knows what he's doing. After all, he chose this one, and then set things up so that, after successfully leaving most of the luns behind by cutting the bridge, that same flen tumbled straight off his horse and down the canyon!"

Some of the flens muttered their agreement, but most of them were more compassionate, and were only really thinking of how to pull their unfortunate comrade out of the mess that he was in.

Levi spoke calmly, but with a hint of irritation.

"I would first like to remind you all of how much we have already gotten through. We have all gathered and have traveled this far, against all odds, as you have just seen. We now have proof that Dominum's son is watching over us, and has even put himself between us and our foes. It is very possible that we might not be here right now if it wasn't for him. I think all of us could see how bad the situation was getting. But here we all are, alive and well, and we also have all of our horses, something to be thankful for. And I must remind you that Nigeb is not dead, something else that is against all odds.

"Furthermore, I would not be so quick to doubt Dominum's son. *He* was there when Erandin was created by his father, *he* knows exactly how this world runs, and *he* sees plainly what is incomprehensible to us. *He* was also sent by his father, quite per-sonally. I believe that all things happen for a purpose, even if it doesn't seem so. I will remind you all again that Dominum's son just saved us, and now I hope that there is no doubt about him. In the meantime, I would like to save Nigeb."

That quieted some of the more displeased flens, and also gave them something to think about.

In the meantime, Thon was coming up with a plan. He could now see clearly that the bridge was too far away from Nigeb to be of any use, but had gone through some of the flens' luggage and found several ropes and a pulley, which they suspended from the branch of a tree that grew there.

They were eventually able to heave up an exhausted and thor-oughly unhappy Nigeb, still clutching his sword.

When the others saw it, they all gathered round him, con-gratulating him at his find, and marveling at the sword and how it had ended up on the ledge. Nigeb explained that it was Yar's sword, and that he had seen it fall. This made them even more interested in it.

After patting each other on the backs and giving out high fives, they all mounted onto their horses, and hurriedly rode off through the mountains and towards the forest that awaited them ahead, with the sun setting to the west. They knew that they weren't in the clear yet.

Chapter 6

Into the Forest

THE FLENS RODE THROUGH the mountains and hills near the canyon quickly. They were still worried about the luns catching up with them, and they certainly did not wish to have anything to do with them.

After they left the South Bridge behind, they could finally breathe easier. Several of them did the calculations and figured that the luns would have to travel far to the west before they could find a way across the long canyon and the Forest River. By then, the flens would be long gone.

The land over which the flens rode steadily became more even and flat, with fields and prairies.

After a full day's ride, the flens now had a good view of the forest that lay ahead. Levi assured them that it was not nearly as big or dark as the one they had already gotten lost in, but there was quite a lot of grumbling among the flens. They knew that this forest was more likely to be populated, whether by beast or human, and were not happy about their chances of meeting someone they did not want to.

As Nigeb rode on his horse, up front next to Levi, he kept thinking about all that had happened during this journey. Of all the books he had read and of all the stories and adventures he had heard of, none of them were even close to this one. And Nigeb thought, *What does this mean? There has to be a meaning after all! And how is this going to end? What's going to happen?* So many questions and not enough answers. Nigeb couldn't help but wonder.

As they rode farther, the flens became quieter. They had nothing to talk about, and were thinking about the forest and all that might happen to them yet. They were relieved to finally leave the fields behind them.

Before them was the beginning of the forest. The forest looked dark and lonely, but the flens didn't have any other choice. They spent the night on the outskirts of the forest, found a path in the morning, and began riding through it, with the sun rising to their left.

Up and down the hills they went. Under trees and over fallen trees their path led. There was little sound in the forest, and the footsteps of the flens' horses rang out rather loudly. It was hard to tell the difference between this forest and the last one, despite what Levi had said, and the rustling of leaves made them uncomfortable.

It became darker as the sun set. The flens were now weary and wished for a break. But they all didn't like the look of the forest anymore, and they didn't dare rest there.

Presently, they came to a stream where they were able to take a drink and fill their bottles. The stream was clear and shallow and the flens were able to cross it without a problem, gently leading their horses until they came to the other side.

As they went on, several flens talked about tales concerning the forest. Stories about luns and wild beasts, and dark spirits and ghosts, and other equally dreadful things that haunted the deepest, darkest ends of the forests, things that loved the dark and hated the light. Anything wretched and evil that served the Hondaloom was bound to be found here. Most especially frightening were the evil wolves that were said to live deep down in the forest. They hated fire, lived in packs, and were dreadfully smart and wicked. They would devour anything and everything until all the light and goodness of it was gone.

Nigeb was bitterly disgusted upon hearing this, and begged that the talker (usually Athor) would stop.

After the sun had already set behind the trees, the flens came to a river. It marked the first half of the forest. This also meant that they were in the deepest part of the forest at night.

The branches of the trees along the banks of the river grew low to the ground, and Nigeb told himself that anyone who tried to ride there had to be careful not to be swept off of their horse by one of the larger branches.

The river itself was deep and fierce, and the flens had to look for a better place to cross, as the path ended abruptly. There was no sign of any bridge or boat, and most of the flens begged Levi to stay on the path. But Levi would not hear of it. He pointed out that it was unwise to stay on the path and sleep, and that they certainly could not go back the way they had come. So the flens shut their mouths and opened their senses and off the path they went.

They rode along the river, their horses stumbling on the uneven bank, until they found a bridge. It was made of wood and was in the shape of an arch. But it was old and musty smelling.

The flens didn't think twice about it, assuming that it had to be better than the rope-constructed South Bridge.

They began to cross the bridge, but as they did so, something terrible happened.

The bridge was not only old but wet and rotten. The flens didn't realize that the bridge could not hold them all up. It was a long bridge and the flens were in a hurry, so that at one point or another they were all on it as they crossed in single file. With all that weight, eight horses, eight flens, and all those bags, the bridge just couldn't do it. It gave way and everyone fell down into the river.

All except for Nigeb.

Nigeb was at the end of the line, so he and his horse were only stepping onto the bridge when it fell. Nigeb's horse had just enough time to turn around and jump off it.

There was a great noise in the forest that night as the bridge crashed into the water. The horses neighed and splashed around, trying to get out, and the flens were yelling and shouting insults at bridge makers in general (the flens did not, after all, have very good experiences with bridges those few days), and trying to get the horses under control without letting the bags float away and without themselves drowning in the process. It would not have been surprising if the whole forest was awake in two minutes.

Nigeb's horse was acting like it was worse off than the others. It snorted and stomped and then charged back into the forest.

Nigeb was trying to gain control over it, and didn't notice the large oak branch in his path until it nailed him in the head.

He remembered nothing after that.

***

When Nigeb came back to his senses, he had a throbbing headache. He was surprised that he was still on horseback, and that he had somehow stayed on in his slumped position. The horse was now quietly walking, and they were in the middle of the forest, all alone. It was very dark, but the full moon was just coming out from behind the clouds, and it lighted the night sky.

Nigeb's first reaction was to swear that he would never ride on a horse again, due to falling off one on the South Bridge, and then falling off one *off* the South Bridge, and then nearly getting decapitated while riding on one. But he quickly realized that it would be an unwise decision, especially since he was riding on one now, and would much rather have it this way than have to walk alone through the forest late at night.

Nigeb then looked around. He nearly fell off his horse. He stared hard into the darkness, trying to find the flens or any sign of their presence. But the forest was deathly silent.

Nigeb had no idea how far he had gotten off track, and he wondered if the flens had noticed his disappearance. Since they had been in the middle of the forest before he got lost, Nigeb assumed that he could be in any part of it by now.

"Levi! . . . Thon! . . . Firm! . . . Oser! . . . Athor! . . . Kevin! . . . Tenzin! Where are you? Can you hear me?!" Nigeb called out, cupping his hands around his mouth to make his voice louder. But there was no answer.

Sweat poured down Nigeb's face, so that he had to constantly wipe it away. He pulled his cloak around as close as he could, seemingly to keep out some unknown cold, and urged his horse forward.

But you must know, dear reader, that it seemed no matter what situation Nigeb got into, he was always able to get out of it, and if you pay close attention as you read this book, you will be able to see what I mean. Nigeb was right when he thought that the evil Hondaloom did not want the flens to reach Flenvinhum. Indeed, though the flens didn't know it, there was a great good among them that the forces of evil wanted to vanquish.

Nigeb's horse seemed to be uneasy, too. It would constantly look from side to side or sniff the air. Nigeb strained his ears, trying to pick up a sound, but all was still.

The young flen made himself stop and calm down. And then he suddenly started to fight with himself. No, not with his fists and his sword, not on the outside but on the inside. Part of him urged to totally lose it, to go tearing through the forest as fast as he could in hope of finding the flens or the end of the forest, or just to lie down and die.

But the other part fought back, telling him to calm down, to gain control over himself, and to stay loyal to his purpose and the flens, and not to give up even if the walls crashed in.

Nigeb didn't know what to do. He was tempted to do option one, the mad rampaging through the forest, but he knew that option two was the right thing to do. He slowly shook his head from side to side, trying to get the evil out of his head. He took a couple of deep breaths and smiled because he had regained control over himself. He closed his eyes and then quickly reopened them.

He slowly moved forward, hoping to eventually find a way out, so that he might be able to reunite with the flens. It seemed the only thing he could do.

There was no sound in the forest, except for his own breathing and that of his horse. This went on for about ten minutes.

Suddenly, Nigeb held his breath. He had seen a shadow behind a tree. The shadow quickly disappeared.

Nigeb didn't have enough time to see what is was, but the shadow was the size of a huge dog. He couldn't tell where the creature went, but he heard sort of a growling and gurgling sound, like a noise coming from deep within a large creature's throat.

Then something jumped at Nigeb from the shadows. The young flen fell off his horse (for the third time), and watched the creature pursue the horse into the forest.

A sharp howl pierced the night. A shadow rose up from behind several rocks, and leaped at Nigeb.

The creature pinned him down by one paw, and the young flen came face to face with a terrible wolf.

It was the biggest wolf Nigeb had ever seen, and seemed bigger than the shadow he had spotted. It growled and bared its teeth. Nigeb was quite helpless at the moment, his sword being in his sheath, which Levi had helpfully provided, as the sword hadn't come with one.

Nigeb then realized that there were more wolves. Another two wolves appeared out of nowhere and began to circle the young flen and the wolf that had pinned him down. Nigeb knew that if he moved he would be torn apart in a matter of seconds, so he stayed as still as is physically possible, wondering why the wolf hadn't eaten him yet.

The look on the wolf's face was a curious and puzzled expression, and Nigeb guessed that it was surprised to find anyone in the forest at all, especially during the night.

The other wolves also looked confused and took turns sniffing Nigeb. What they really didn't like and what made them growl the most was his sword.

The wolf that had pinned Nigeb down began to growl loudly, and he could sense the feeling of death coming from it. With a huge pounce it leaped into the air.

That was a mistake, because when it leaped, Nigeb had just enough time to get out of the way, so that the wolf bit the ground instead of him.

The flen jumped to his feet: some great power had taken hold of him. He quickly drew his sword and with one swing cut off the wolf's head.

The other wolves leaped at Nigeb, mouths open, teeth bared, legs outstretched, claws ready to tear apart anything that was in their way, all focusing on one particular flen.

Nigeb stood tall, legs apart, ready for anything. He didn't feel helpless anymore, but felt brave and courageous, and a bit frightened. One after the other the two wolves leaped at Nigeb, and one after the other they both fell before him.

But Nigeb had scarcely killed the second wolf when two more showed up. One jumped toward him but didn't make it. The other one felt cold steel before it had a chance to attack.

Five more wolves appeared out of the shadows, and when they had just begun to close in, another one came leaping over the fallen trees.

Nigeb didn't know how many wolves he faced and killed that day. It seemed that for every wolf he killed, two more came. For a while, he counted the wolves but had to stop at around twenty, and still many more came after that. That day, Nigeb killed almost all the wolves that lived in the forest, and all the rest fled and never came back. Many years later that forest would be named the forest of Wolf's Fear, and if you are ever being chased by wolves and happen to be near it, all you have to do is go into the forest, for the wolves fear it and will not go into it. And that is why there are no wolves in the forest of Wolf's Fear.

Finally, there was nothing but dead wolves left. At first, Nigeb wasn't so sure about that and just quietly stood there, waiting to suddenly be pounced on. But two minutes went by and no wolf came, five minutes went by and still nothing, ten minutes went by and finally Nigeb was convinced.

He felt so unstoppable and courageous that he just about forgot that he was still in the middle of the forest.

When he realized this, that sinking feeling returned. He knew that he was in the same situation as before, but tried to remind himself that he was still alive and had proven himself a greater warrior than he had ever thought he was.

"I would give a lot to be home right now, where it is safe and cozy, and in bed, filled with supper. Away with these cursed forests, the heck with them!" Nigeb said, thinking about the last time he had a meal, which was midday yesterday.

All he could do now was go out into the dark forest and try to find either the flens or a way out. Nigeb wiped his sword on the grass, put it in its sheath and carefully went through the forest.

The forest was once again deathly silent, and the howling and sounds of the wolves seemed a distant memory. But Nigeb still remained cautious, half expecting something to jump at him from behind a tree or bush. He was no longer on a path, and all he could do was guess the direction of the river or the way out and go in as straight of a line as possible.

"Okay," Nigeb said to himself. "When I was still with the flens, and still on the path, and still near the river, what kind of trees were there? Were they elms? No wait, they weren't, they were . . . were they oaks? Yes! That's it! They were oaks! And there were many of them and they were tall, yes I remember! It was an oak branch that cracked me on the head, after all.

"So right now, in order to find the path, I need to look for oaks." Nigeb looked around but he didn't see any oaks or anything that resembled them.

"All right, what else was there?" he asked himself. "I do remember that the ground around the path was bare and there weren't any plants or stones . . . but the ground here is boiling with plants." He looked in the direction of his feet, which were hidden in plants and foliage up to his knees.

"I must be in the wrong place. Oh, how big is this forest? It must go on for miles and I don't even know which way I'm going!"

Nigeb looked up at the moon—it was in the middle of the dark sky. The young flen heard something behind him. He whipped his head around to see an owl fly off. Nigeb gripped his sword and put on the hood of his cloak. He felt more confident this way. As if that could scare off his fears, which seemed to know exactly where he was and what he was doing.

Upon coming into a more open part of the forest, Nigeb blindly ran forward at a great speed, as only flens can do, with the grass and weeds whipping at his legs and holding him back. He nearly tripped once or twice on a root or a rock that had been hidden in the foliage. But he managed to stay upright and reached his destination in about ten minutes.

He had come to a more dark part of the forest, and he stayed at the edge for a considerable amount of time, wondering whether or not he should go in. But with a sudden yelp, he realized that the trees in front of him were oaks, tall and ancient, with twisted branches and enormous roots that came out of the ground.

Nigeb plunged in without a second thought, hoping desperately that he would get to safety after all.

He weaved around the trees, moving from side to side, hoping to get a better idea of where the path could be, until he exhausted himself.

And that's when he noticed that the ground was bare, smooth, and dusty. He nearly jumped up and down from excitement, and then raced off towards that direction. He realized how scared he felt, now that he was so close, and could almost feel the tension of the forest. He thought about what had happened to him in the forest so far, and hoped that his adventures here were over.

After getting tired all over again, and running a good distance as well, he finally saw the path!

With great excitement, Nigeb jumped down on the path. He still remembered that he had only found the path and that he still didn't know where his friends were, but he couldn't help feeling safe again.

After a moment, he realized that he didn't know which direction to go. He had no idea whether to go up the path or down it, which was a problem, because if he went in the wrong direction, he'd end up at the wrong side of the forest, separated from his friends and possibly in danger from the luns.

Nigeb ran up and down the path, blaming himself for not thinking of this, and then he began to bend down occasionally to look for tracks. The ground was dusty and bare, and rock-hard. There was no sign of any horses passing by, or anything else for that matter.

There was no sound of running water either, which meant the river was not at hand.

Imagine the poor, lost, almost eaten flen's excitement when he finally found a single horse hoof imprint towards the side of the path. It was pointing up the path, and Nigeb sped in that direction quicker than thinking. He could only hope that the imprint was pointing in the right direction, and that the horse hadn't been facing the wrong way when it was made.

But his hopes proved right when he began to hear the sound of running water. In several minutes he arrived at the river bank and this time he could be certain where he needed to go.

Reluctantly, he jumped off the path, and then made his way to where the bridge had stood.

The water was just as angry and dangerous as before, but Nigeb grabbed a chunk of the bridge which had drifted to shore, and jumped into the water.

He made it to the other side, but not before drifting farther downriver and having to vigorously fight to stay afloat and get to the other side alive.

As soon as he got out, he went back up river to see if he could find the flens. But he could not find them or any evidence of them. The full picture of the frightful situation that he was in finally dawned on him. The flens could be anywhere on this side of the forest, or worse, they could still be on the other side. After all, Nigeb assumed that they had come out on this side of the river after their accident, but he could have been wrong.

Nigeb began to walk along the river. He figured that the flens would probably set up camp somewhere hidden and then go looking for him, so he decided to look for a good camp site where his friends might be. But he was drenched, cold, hungry, and over all miserable. He wondered why he had come on this journey in the first place, having had to risk his life a good four times at least (during the fight with the luns, when he fell off the South Bridge, when he was attacked by wolves, and when he almost drowned swimming across the river).

Nigeb searched in the bushes and the undergrowth, and even climbed a few trees in hope of seeing something, but for a while he couldn't find anything. He wondered if his friends were desperately searching for him, or if they had given up and moved on. He couldn't believe all the trouble he had gotten into.

Nigeb was starting to give up. He had found a path, a very small one that winded up farther into the forest, but he didn't have the heart to follow it, or think what could have possibly made it. He slumped against a tree, and had nearly fallen asleep when he saw a twinkle of light up ahead.

He got up as fast as he could, wiping the sleep from his eyes. He staggered up the path, towards the light. Thinking that it was the flens, he almost yelled out to them, but found that he was too exhausted to. Thank goodness.

As he stumbled nearer, he heard voices, loud and gruff, and realized at once that they didn't match the more smooth voices of flens.

Nigeb got down on all fours and crept up and peered over some bushes. To his great fear and surprise, it was not the flens. It was several luns.

They were sitting on logs around a campfire, and roasting something over it on tongs. There were three of them, but they were exceptionally small for luns. Nigeb realized at once that they were the less vicious and dangerous kind of dwarf luns, not Yar and his warriors.

He saw that the luns were sitting in front of a big hut, so he guessed that they lived there. But how they managed he could not tell (little did he know of the skill and usefulness of a dwarf lun in the forest. They are excellent at survival and have a way unknown to man at living in the wilderness. They are, however, completely isolated, and can be dangerous, although not as vicious as the other luns. They also happen to be a bit dim, and have a rough way of talking). Their house was surrounded by dense forest on all sides, the type which you could walk thirty steps into and then never find your way out again. The only area clear of trees was the small patch of dirt that they were sitting on.

Nigeb understood quite well now the dangers and wildness of the forest he was in, and therefore remained quiet. He decided to listen to their conversation and see if he could learn of a way out, or if they were safe enough to talk to.

The luns' conversation was quite strange. One of them was earnestly telling the other two something.

"Did you hear the mountains rumble? Did you hear the oceans rage? Did you feel the forest tremble? Did you hear the flens cry out? The doom of evil is coming!" he whispered to the other luns. Nigeb caught a glint of his eyes, and they weren't that of a lunatic or liar.

"Ha! Who told yer that!? Besides, how do we know who, good or evil, is going to win? Seems to me that both sides are equally matched, that is. Yer always one to be weird, Lukisium." the second lun said, and then snorted. He bit into whatever was being cooked, seemed to choke on it, and started coughing. He then put it back into the fire.

"Who told me it, you ask, Sim?" the first lun, Lukisium, said. "'Bout time some sense was knocked into your noggin. I said I heard the mountains rumble, you dork. And I don't care if the sides are equally matched, because they ain't. That Hondaloom was *created* by Dominum, and the creator is always greater than the creation. That's before he became evil and all—what was Dominum thinking? And I said the doom of evil is coming. Key word, *doom.*"

"Dork yourself," Sim said. "Yer gone crazy, yer know. Now hurry up and help me with this pork, or else it'll burn and yer be left without supper, doom of stomach I'll say. Careful! Careful! Yer burning the meat, dork."

"You are the dork, because I called you one first, whether you like it or not." Lukisium shot back. "Or how does dimwit apply to yer? What about mister glutton? I'm telling yer about the doom of evil!"

"Well, how about, 'did yer hear the bacon burn'? You set fire to it! And the doom of evil does not exist. Same with Dominum and that Hondaloom."

Well, Nigeb thought. *How come I saw Dominum's son, and firsthand experienced that he is real? He did cut the bridge in half after all! And it only took a second. That bridge was no good, but the ropes it was made of were too thick for someone to cut them like that. And, after all, isn't there more proof in someone saying that Dominum's son exists because they saw him firsthand than someone saying that Dominum's son doesn't exist just because they haven't seen him? And if Dominum's son exists, then certainly doesn't Dominum and the evil Hondaloom exist as well?!*

Right at that time, the third lun spoke up. He had a high voice and Nigeb had a difficult time understanding him.

"I say, what're we gon do when this doom of evil feller shows up? We good guys, or we bad guys . . . or we good guys?"

"Oh, come on Squeaky, we're talking about serious stuff, like supper, which Lukisium is burning." Sim mumbled under his breath.

Lukisium blew ecstatically on the meat, which was now ablaze, tong and all.

"I am with the doom of evil, certainly." he grumbled, and tossed the tong into the fire. "I don't believe you would follow the evil Hondaloom, either."

But the lun with the high voice wasn't listening. He was indignant because Sim had called him Squeaky. His name was not Squeaky!

"Name not Squeaky! Name Skeeter!" he shrieked, his face turning red.

The other two luns howled with laughter, but they weren't laughing when Skeeter broke a wooden tray over Sim's head.

"Yow!" Sim howled. "How dare you! You degraded pig!"

Skeeter hopped on a log to make himself look taller, and screamed with all his lungs, his face now bright red. "How dare you?!"

"Silence!" Lukisium yelled, louder than both of them, pounding his fist on a stump.

Everything was absolutely quiet. Then the three luns started mumbling insults at each other, such as "fatty," "pig," and "ninny."

"Will you stop it already!" Lukisium shouted, right after he called Sim a dork with asthma.

"Yer the one who started it," Sim replied, rubbing his head. "It's yer fault yer insist on lying all the time."

Suddenly, the front door of the hut burst open and out came a fourth lun, carrying a tray with food and drinks.

"What are yer lying about?" he shouted.

"Nothing, nothing," muttered Lukisium.

"I still wanna know!" shouted the lun.

"I was just telling them what I told yer, Kael." Lukisium answered him.

Kael chuckled and said something out of Nigeb's hearing range.

Then the luns sat down and began to talk of things and events of late. At first, they were interesting and exciting, conversations about the wilderness and about the way of things. They were quite knowledgeable when it came to things like this.

But soon they began to talk of things of no sense to Nigeb, and he was quickly lost to their conversation.

He had been so caught up in the luns' conversation that he had forgotten that he was still lost, and that he still didn't know where his friends were, and when he realized this, he decided to get going.

He tried to carefully creep away but to his absolute horror he stumbled forward and crashed face-first into the bushes ahead of him, making an impressive racket.

The luns were up and ready in a second.

"Dark Ghost if I'm not stupid." Sim yelled, sweeping an axe off the ground. Nigeb had not noticed it before.

"Probably an unwanted intruder." Kael shouted back, and brandished a long carving knife. "And yer are stupid. Bless me if it isn't a spy of the Hondaloom, listening to yer talking."

Lukisium and Skeeter grabbed burning tongs, and all four of them went out into the forest in search of the unlikely intruder.

Nigeb scrambled to his feet, and ran blindly back into the forest. It was the last place he ever wanted to go, but it was hard for him to see any other options.

He fled through the forest, now almost pitch black except for the faint glow of the full moon, which was mostly blocked out by the trees.

Shouts went up as the luns chased after him. But they weren't as fast as he was, not with their short legs and full bellies. Their navigation was far better than his, and they could see him and hear him. But they were relieved that it wasn't a Dark Ghost that they were dealing with, and they were contented with just giving whoever it was a good scare. So after a while they stopped their pursuit and went back.

But Nigeb didn't appreciate this "kindness." He ran as fast as he could, and when he crashed into trees, or fell into bushes, he got up and stumbled forward almost as soon as he made contact with the ground, not daring to stop or even look back.

He suddenly came to the edge of a very steep hill with a large incline. He lost his footing on the loose rocks and went tumbling down the hillside.

But when he stopped going round in circles and came back to his senses, he realized that he was standing in the midst of his friends! Of course there was a lot of happiness and rejoicing and the flens were all relieved that they were finally back together.

Then they insisted on Nigeb telling them about how he got lost and about what he did and how he felt.

Nigeb told them about passing out and waking up to find himself alone; he also told them of the wolves and about how he battled them. He frighteningly described seeing the wolf's shadow before he was attacked, and he told them of how he was looking for them and then came across the luns. He told them about the conversation he heard, especially the part about the doom of evil.

When he told them this, Levi got a faraway look, and Nigeb wondered what it was about. Had Levi noticed something that he hadn't?

When Nigeb was finished, the flens in their turn told him about how they all fell into the river and how it took them a long time to get back together and how they quickly realized that Nigeb was missing and how they split up to go look for him but couldn't succeed and how they all got back together, after almost getting helplessly lost, to decide what to do next and how Nigeb had suddenly come out of nowhere.

Levi just nodded the whole time and seemed to be deep in thought.

Finally, he patted Nigeb on the shoulder and said. "I am happy to have you back, Nigeb. You have proved to be more resourceful and courageous than we thought at first, and I am happy to have you along with us. We may need you yet."

After that, the flens set out at once, with Nigeb riding along with Kevin, as he didn't have his own horse now. Another full day of riding brought them to the edge of the forest, and before the night began, they rode out of the darkness and into the open fields ahead.

Chapter 7

Almost There Now

THE FLENS JOURNEYED THROUGH the next day, and finally
came to a village that was inhabited by humans.

It was a small village, surrounded on all sides by a tall, wood-
en fence, proving that the area they lived in was untamed.

The flens got in easily, although they were greeted by several
guards. The flens were informed that the lands were getting more
dangerous as the seasons went by, and the guards warned them of
the danger of luns. It was old news but the flens were reminded by
Levi to stay on guard. It would be dangerous for them to fall into
the hands of Yar and his warriors.

The flens had several jokes regarding Yar and his luns. Mostly
about them taking a swim in the Forest River to freshen up their
bad smell. They were still relieved about getting through the forest
safely, and their spirits were high.

Of course, on the inside, they were all afraid of the luns.

Nigeb was still somewhat delirious from his experience in the
woods and was shaken up from being chased by the dwarf luns
at the very end of his adventure. But coming to safety was a great
comfort and also a relief. The flens' supplies were getting dangerously low, and the wild landscape around didn't provide much ed-
ible things.

As soon as they had refilled and restocked their provisions, the flens continued from the village and through the landscape. After traveling a few dreary and long days, during which nothing interesting happened and they began to once again get low on supplies, they finally came to the beginnings of the White Mountain.

The landscape around the outskirts of the mountain was lush and fruitful. It was a warm welcome compare to the lands the flens had had to endure.

It was bright and green. Plenty of trees and plants grew here, right along the path that the flens followed.

Due to it still being summer, not everything was ripe, but nothing stopped the flens from plucking fruit right off the trees as they rode along.

Soon the bubbling and gurgling of a stream was heard, and they came to a large stream with clear and clean water. The water was sweet, and the flens were very much uplifted. The prospect of reaching Flenvinhum didn't seem quite so far away.

The White Mountain loomed not too far above them, and beyond that was a settlement area, and farther south, but not too far, was a string of mountains that they would follow to Flenvinhum. So far, there wasn't a sign of the luns, and the flens were beginning to hope that they had lost them permanently.

Nigeb was perhaps the most uneasy about this, because he couldn't be quite sure whether or not the luns knew their destination was in Flenvinhum. After all, if the luns knew where the flens would be, what was keeping them from showing up sooner or later? Levi, however, assured Nigeb that Dominum's son would be there, and that it would be far more difficult for the luns to harm them in the flens' capital city than it would be in the wilderness.

Nigeb wasn't quite so sure and tried not to think about the isolation of the wilderness they were currently in. So far, they hadn't seen any signs of people outside of the village they had stopped in, and they wouldn't until they reached the settlements on the other side of the White Mountain.

The upward journey was perilous. The rough and rocky landscape beyond the green, pleasant meadows at the foot of the mountain was dangerously unstable for their horses. It was smoldering hot and stuffy, but the flens were more worried about the icy slopes and snowy peaks that they would soon be crossing.

Several flens (primarily Thon and Firm) had wondered whether they could go around the mountain, but Levi assured them that it would take too long, and that they were far more likely to encounter hostile luns should they go around.

Of course, that convinced everyone. But the question of successfully making it over with their horses and luggage still remained.

I must say that though they had many hard situations and many problems, they were able to cross over the mountain in the end. They found a path that all the horses could travel by, and though they lost it several times, they were able to find it again each time. Sometimes the path became icy or covered in snow, and then they would have to find a way around or send out a scout on skis, but they all made it through alive. And it might as well have been winter, so snowy was the mountain.

In the end, they descended down the other side, and entered the green valley below during the evening of the day after starting up the mountain.

It was a warm welcome to be in summer weather once again. The flens were a little shaken up from tackling the mountain, but were pleased to have all made it. They were also eager to make it to the settlements before nightfall.

Fortunately, the edge of the settlements was not far off. And after riding swiftly through the valley and several miles or so on more rough landscape, a town came into view.

It was certainly larger than the one they had gone through before ascending the mountain. It was positioned on a dip in the landscape, and the flens had a bird's eye view of the town.

It was large and stretched out far along the fields. It had a low fence along its perimeter, and towards the center was a marketplace. In the distance beyond it could be seen rows and rows of fields and crops, with the occasional farm and road. Farther south could be seen outlines of more settlements, including towns and farms.

The flens had finally reached the edge of the Land of Onar! They had made it through the Wilderness, through forests and over mountains, and were finally entering the lands that would lead them to Flenvinhum.

After the flens rode down the dip, they came none too soon to the gates. There they were met with more welcome than before. There were certainly fewer guards, and they were more friendly, almost trusting. They had far fewer problems with characters such as luns, unlike the lands on the other side of the White Mountain.

The flens were informed that they were less than three days' journey from reaching Flenvinhum, and that they could reach the marketplace, where they would be restocked on provisions.

Apparently, there was a festival, and the flens soon noticed that when they tried to get through the streets of swarming farmers and villagers, while riding on horseback.

It was well into the evening. The flens had many problems finding a place to sleep, the inns being full. But they finally found an inn that had one last open room, which all eight of them had to share.

***

Nigeb woke up the next morning feeling refreshed. It was the first decent night he had since leaving Ullantown, and sleeping up on the White Mountain had been terrible.

"I see no use in trying to do anything at this time of day." Levi stated at the quick breakfast. Some of the flens had been asking about whether or not they should do some final preparations and head out. "It is bound to be crowded this morning, that with all the villagers rushing to get who-knows-where during this festival."

The flens didn't set out until late afternoon. They hoped to have lunch somewhere (as they had not had a decent meal for a while now) and stock up on provisions before leaving to complete the easier part of their journey.

The sun was high up in the sky, and it was uncomfortably hot.

The flens led their horses through the busy streets and bought all their provisions, nearly running out of money (Oser wasn't happy and complained loudly about being bled dry by the adventure).

The flens finally reached the back gate, where they left their horses. They themselves went in search of a place where they could eat.

The flens saw a sign for a restaurant, and they decided to stop there.

It was not a very fancy restaurant, and it was very crowded. The flens managed to push through and get to the front, but not before meeting some very strange persons, some of which were drunk, or at least something like that.

Nigeb was bumped into several times by people who looked like they didn't know where they were going. Athor nearly got into a scuffle, and Oser had to push people out of the way.

There was a man standing on a table. He had a full beard and a dark face, and didn't look sober. At first he sang, and when nothing came out of it because he couldn't get anything to rhyme, he started to talk about science, but he got everything wrong.

After ordering their meal, the flens sat down to their first satisfying meal in a week.

I must say that the food was delicious, although not much can be expected from a restaurant such as the one they were in. Their meal consisted of mostly bread and cheese and a mix of meat. Corn and salad was also added as it was a good year for crops. The flens also enjoyed a sweet, nutty, milky beverage similar to eggnog, although not as sugar-filled.

The flens talked fondly of their adventures, and Thon spoke of making a book entitled: *The Odyssey From Ullantown To Flenvinhum*. It would be centered around their adventures so far, and hopefully would end in them reaching Flenvinhum (but that's only how he *thought* it would end).

At the end of their meal, Nigeb got up and started towards the door. But as he lifted up his personal bag, which he had brought along, the satchel with his father's map fell out. The satchel rolled away, and came to rest at the feet of a large man.

He picked it up momentarily and looked inside.

Before Nigeb could stop him, the map was unrolled on a table, and the man was studying it.

After a moment, the man looked over and said. "A flen! Strange to see one of you in a place like this, instead of one of your castles in Flenvinhum!" Then he added gruffly, "What price do you want for it?"

Nigeb clenched his teeth. "It's not for sale."

By now the rest of the flens were on their feet, and Athor moved towards the man.

The man slapped his hand down on the map, as if saying that he would not be persuaded to give it up so easily.

Athor grabbed the satchel and said, "He said it's not for sale."

Several men moved in next to the big man. Pushing between the flens and men started, and the big man started staring threateningly at Nigeb.

Athor suddenly threw the satchel up at the man's face. Both of the man's hands momentarily went up to catch it, and Athor flipped over the table, grabbed the map, and then rolled off the other side! He dove under a table as a large brute reached for him, and reappeared on the other side.

By now, all havoc had been released upon the dining room. Open fights were starting. Random objects were thrown through the air. Tables and chairs were overturned.

Levi ducked under a swung chair, and then the chair knocked an assailant behind him unconscious.

Oser was being a good example and yelling for a moment of attention so that they could discuss matters like decent, civilized people (or, in his case, flens). But things fell apart when, out of nowhere, a plate came crashing down on his head. He stumbled and fell backwards into the man who had hit him. Both of them fell on a table, and the man got a face full of pie. Oser jumped up quick as lightning and two more men attacked him. He dodged one and made the other one trip but he himself tripped and fell over, kicking and throwing punches all the way to the floor.

Athor sensed that it was time to wrap things up. He threw his shoulder into his opponent like a real football player, knocking him to the ground. With powerful strides, he charged towards the table with the big, troublemaking man. Athor gracefully flipped over the table, snatched the satchel out of the big man's hands, and then slid the map into it before landing on the other side. Then, with a loud yell of, "Nigeb!" he tossed it through the air in a clean spiral.

Nigeb saw the satchel coming, dodged his opponent, and snatched it out of the air.

Then his opponent bumped into him, causing him to lose his balance.

But just as he was about to fall back, firm hands grabbed his shoulders and heaved him back to his feet.

Nigeb spun his head in time to see Levi change his grip in order to pull him to the side.

"We need to get out of here!" Levi yelled. The flens were now retreating. Oser made it to the front of the restaurant and burst open the door.

"This way!" he yelled frantically, and then disappeared outside.

Several flens made it outside, dodging angry opponents. Firm dove through the door in his fright, and managed to land on Tenzin, who tumbled down the street. Levi pushed Nigeb outside (who was still clutching the satchel) and then slammed the door shut behind them.

Nigeb and Levi raced down to the gates where the other flens were already waiting. Some of them were tattered, and Oser had several bruises, although I can assure you that he dealt out many more than he received. Fortunately, no casualties were present, and the only thing the flens wanted clear was why the man wanted the map.

But Nigeb could only shrug, as he himself was still guessing.

They had not been chased, but they did not linger. The flens hurriedly mounted their horses and rode away through the back gates and into the beautiful, green country beyond.

Their destination was now so close.

Chapter 8

Dominum's Son

NEEDLESS TO SAY, THE next two days of journeying were unexciting for the flens. Now they rode through fields and towns, over civilized lands and past cultivated people, making more progress on the well-looked-after roads than ever before.

Their last day of travel was the most interesting, as they finally neared Flenvinhum and could now see the outskirts and even the walls of the magnificent city, where everything was green and prosperous and the flens dwelled in splendor and the king sat on his High Throne. Even small, colorful dragons were said to be seen flying through the sky.

The city stretched from horizon to horizon, with walls and towers seemingly reaching the sky, and countless red, orange, and yellow flags, the national color of flens, flapping rapidly in the wind. The city itself sat on a high hill, surrounded by a deep trench. A wide road led up the hill, over the drawbridge, and right to the gates waiting magnificently on top. The city was well-protected but was just as friendly if you came with good intentions.

The flens gallantly rode through the gates, swelling with pride at seeing the city of their people. Nigeb, who had never been outside Ullantown up until now, was quite dazzled. He gazed with wonder at the towering walls and at the smooth, shiny surface of their stonework. The feeling was quite hard to explain, but Nigeb felt as though he was at the top of the world.

The other flens were also feeling quite pleased, and proud, to have made it through everything to finally arrive at the city of their destination.

As soon as they entered the gates, they quickly encountered the busyness and wholesomeness of the community. Everywhere on the main road, flens hustled about, smiling and calling out greetings, and going to and fro about their business. Shops and buildings lined the streets, and you could find adventure anywhere you turned. Everything seemed bright and exciting, and the flens were beaming as they dismounted their horses and began exploring.

Nigeb was fascinated by the buildings and architecture, which was advanced in that time and day. The stone roads were well-paved and looked after, the buildings were inviting and brightly colored, and the parks and public squares were cheerful.

Indeed, for the next week, Nigeb heard very little from his fellow flens, as each seemed to be engaged in whatever it was he was doing.

✳✳✳

Nigeb had wandered about Flenvinhum for days, and had gotten more accustomed to it. He had found places to sleep, and plenty of places where to fill his stomach. He had seen and explored many of the interesting memorials and attractions and marvels Flenvinhum had to offer. But in all this, he was wondering about when he would next see his friends, and when they would continue with what they had come there for.

He had given plenty of thought to Dominum's son, and had asked many questions, but it was hard to find anything helpful. All of the flens knew who he was but most had never met him. Those that had had testified that he really was the son of Dominum, and they assured Nigeb that if he wanted to meet Dominum's son, then Dominum's son would meet *him*. All of them said, however, that there was no way to find him on your own.

Then one day, a week after the flens' arrival in Flenvinhum, Nigeb went to the market, hoping to find his friends there. He wandered about the stalls and tents, ignoring the friendly shouts of sellers. However, he could not find his friends or any trace of them.

It was a warm day, about noon. Not a wisp of a cloud in the bright blue sky. Nigeb was able to make out a large mountain looming in the distance. The mountain was behind the city, standing closer to the sea. This was the first time Nigeb had seen it, and he was wondering what it was exactly.

After being in the marketplace, Nigeb went and sat down on the front steps of some little shop, a nice, secluded area where he could think and chew on a piece of straw.

As he sat with his elbow upon his knee and his chin on his knuckles, an old man walked up.

He was very old, yet he had seemed to escape age. He had long white hair and an even longer white beard. He had bushy eyebrows and an olive-skinned face and hands. The rest of him was hidden under a gray cloak. He had a pointed hood on his head, and his right hand held a staff.

Nigeb looked up inquisitively, still chewing the straw.

The old man smiled, and then frowned, his eyebrows drawing together as he peered out at Nigeb as one would out of a hat.

"Good day," Nigeb called out to the stranger. The old man had reminded Nigeb of his adoptive grandfather, who had treated him like his own, and had always fascinated Nigeb with stories of battles and bravery, riches and treasures, stories of heroes and villains, and forces of good and evil.

The man raised an eyebrow, but still managed to keep frowning. "Hmm, let's see, Mr. Nigeb Fortrute, I believe. Now tell me why just a minute ago you seemed to be down in the depths of the ocean, and now you say 'good day'?"

It is no wonder that Nigeb was caught off guard when he heard his full name from a stranger, but he managed to keep a smile on. "It's a beautiful morning, sir, the birds are singing, the sun is shining, and I have much to be thankful for. Just being here is a miracle, considering the circumstances of my journey to this city."

The old man smiled again, his eyebrows back to their normal position.

Nigeb looked at him keenly, trying to recall whatever it was that he now felt. "I don't believe I know your name, sir."

"No, indeed you don't, but I know your name, and I believe you know who I am." the old man replied.

Nigeb was at a loss, but then he thought back to the encounter in Ullantown. "You must be Dominum's son!"

The old man laughed a quiet, deep laugh. "So it is indeed, and I believe that you have found your man. You have come in answer to my calling and now I shall tell you of all things, but only if you are willing."

Nigeb found himself almost laughing. The old man's joy was very contagious. He sprang up to his feet. "I want to know more about *everything* concerning the events that have been happening to me, not to mention my parents."

"Then you must follow me," Dominum's son replied. He gazed up to the mountain looming in the distance. "Follow me to that mountain, and you will learn of everything."

"The mountain!" Nigeb exclaimed, staring at the towering peak. But then his mind changed, and he breathed deeply. "Then take me there, if you must. But first, I would like to know your name."

"Which one? For I have many names." Dominum's son answered.

Nigeb thought about it. "The one that the flens have for you."

"Eranor."

✱✱✱

It was a hot and perilous climb.

Beside his aching mind and limbs, Nigeb was feeling dehydrated and tired. He hadn't expected to have to climb up so high. A steep stone stairway led to the top of the mountain, winding round and round it. But the stairs just went and went.

Eranor seemed unaffected by the sun and the climb. He went quietly and quickly, staying ahead of the flen.

Nigeb would have used this time to ask questions, but he was much too exhausted.

They had hiked from the city, all the way to the base of the mountain, a good two hours or so. Then they had started climbing, with no account for supplies of food, water, or proper gear and attire.

Nigeb would have complained loudly, but you don't usually give the son of Dominum complaints. Also, Nigeb had to remind himself that he agreed to this, and that Eranor had said that he wouldn't take him anywhere unless he was willing.

Either way, Nigeb was on the verge of collapsing when suddenly a steep rock wall on their right fell away, revealing a large building on the very top of the mountain.

They had reached their destination!

Nigeb looked curiously at Eranor. Was this what he wanted to show him? The large building was a surprise to Nigeb: he hadn't expected to see anything here, much less an impressive, beautifully made structure surrounded by a large wall.

When they made their way to the large, fantastically decorated gates, Eranor pushed them open and walked through, saying, "This is the Monastery. It was built when the first flens came into this land, and Flenvinhum started from here. It was inhabited by the family of Ron, the forefather of all flens, and because of this it was given its name. Here the nation that was to resist the power of the Hondaloom was born."

The two walked into a large courtyard, the beginning of the Monastery.

Nigeb and Eranor walked across the courtyard, and entered a pair of double doors.

The doors led to the inside of the Monastery. It was a large, well-built building with many a hallway and many secrets. Large doors led to rooms, great and small, and countless artifacts and scrolls lined the walls on shelves.

But despite all, Nigeb still had one particular question in mind. Pulling out the letter he had received all those weeks ago on a summer morning in Ullantown, the letter that Dominum's son had written, he showed it to Eranor. "This letter says that you would tell me more about my parents, whom I know nothing of, and with all due respect, I am here, in Flenvinhum, just as you requested, and you are here as well, and I have risked head and body climbing this mountain (Eranor gave him a questioning look), and I would like to know more about them."

"Indeed, I am sure you would," Eranor replied. "And I am a keeper of my word. Nigeb, you shall now learn of your father and mother, and know that there is none who could contradict me in my telling.

"Your father, Nigeb, was a good flen. Nilleb Fortrute the Second, whose family came from that of Nilleb the First, the son of Ron, was born here in Flenvinhum as the eldest son of his family. He was especially skilled at mapmaking and charting, and was willing to use his talents. He was a great help to me, and made many a map for the use of his fellow flens.

"He first met me when I rescued him from deep in the Northern Forests, where he had lost his way, despite the map he had. I then gave him a new map, one that would never lead him astray. It was shortly after this that he came to Ullantown, being twenty-three years of age, and where he also met your mother.

"Your father made finding a way to fight the Hondaloom his life's goal. I told him that the time was not right, but he was persistent. I decided to use his talents, and in the right time he made a map, the key to finding a resistance force against the Hondaloom. He very much wanted to find the location on the map and receive the power to fight the Hondaloom, but I told him again that the time was not right. I instructed him that the map was to be given to *you*. He did so, and shortly after he and your mother were killed by luns.

"Your mother was also a flen, but from a different family. She raised you for the first few years of your life, but before that she lived in Flenvinhum and then in Ullantown, where she married your father. She shared in a few of your father's adventures, but she knew me before your father did and it was I that led her to Ullantown."

Nigeb quietly looked at the floor, thinking through what Eranor had said, as he himself had never heard anything like it. He tried to quietly look at Eranor, but was met with those deep eyes and the sad smile.

Eranor beckoned the young flen, and they retraced their path and ended up where they had begun. Sitting on the front stairs of the Monastery, the ones that led up to the gate, Eranor began to whistle, although it was unlike any whistling Nigeb had ever heard. Sweet, soft music began to pour out of his lips, all in the form of whistling, and the wind seemed to dance as it floated back and forth, here and there, spiraling up and down in sync with the notes.

Nigeb put his letter away and listened. They sat like this, just like old friends, until Nigeb stopped and broke the silence by saying, "How could you let this happen? How could you let them go?"

Eranor stopped all at once and looked at Nigeb. "My dear, dear son, it is because I see the past, the present, and the future, like a great painted canvas before my eyes, and I saw what must happen exactly for the Hondaloom to be defeated and for my father, Dominum, to be king once again in Erandin.

"Take heart, Nigeb, son of Nilleb Fortrute! I am here so that one day you may see both your parents in a better place than this."

"A better place?" Nigeb asked.

"Yes, my father's land."

"You mean to say, the place where Dominum is, the place that the Hondaloom and all evil is forever banished from?" Nigeb asked.

"Yes, when the Hondaloom turned against my father, he was banished to roam Erandin, while Dominum separated himself from the evil of this world. Evil is forbidden in his land. But the Hondaloom unrightfully rules Erandin, and that means ultimate death for its people, for he has his death mark upon them, the Great Chasm. But my father wants to redeem the people of this world, so that they could freely live with him in his land. That is why I have come."

"So why did you want me? Why did you call me?" Nigeb asked. He had, after all (and I'm sure that the reader can testify), traversed a vast distance and had to overcome much in order to be sitting there.

"Behold, I am here to put an end to the Hondaloom, and to bring Erandin back!" Eranor cried, rising to his feet. He seemed to grow several feet in a second, and the old man was not recognizable. "I have called you personally so that you might learn to fight the Hondaloom and so that you could witness the great events in store! You have accepted my call, and now I will teach you the way of the Azoons, the warriors of Old! And after I go back to my father's land, you shall be in my place, and shall fight the evil of the Hondaloom until the time will come and the world is made anew! And in your rightful time, you shall go to live in the land of Dominum, along with your fathers and forefathers."

He sat down, now back to his former figure, and added, "Do you accept this proposal?"

"Yes," Nigeb found his voice. "I accept. I have already accepted. I now see that it is my only rightful choice."

"I will fight for you," Dominum's son answered quietly. "You are under my protection now. Your journey here has only just begun. Always look towards the light, Nigeb, son of Nilleb. Now, your father had a diary. You will find it in your new room."

The two rose and went back in, Nigeb now feeling the full weight of his decision. And he felt that he couldn't have made a better choice. There was no turning back, right from the moment that he had followed the letter's directions, and that was perhaps a good thing, for he would need to remember that in the days to come.

Nigeb followed Eranor back inside again, down a long hallway, and to a pair of large double doors.

"These are your living quarters, and this is where you will sleep." Eranor put a hand on the doorknob. "Right now you will get comfortable with your surroundings, and you will also meet with the others."

"There are others?" Nigeb asked. He hadn't quite seen that coming.

Eranor smiled and laughed. "You've forgotten, haven't you? You didn't come to Flenvinhum on your own, did you?"

Eranor turned around and walked back up the hallway, still laughing quietly.

Nigeb pushed the doors open, and found more doors. He counted them, and found that there were eight. He walked up to the one that said *Nigeb,* and then noticed the names on the other doors: *Levi, Athor, Oser.*

Nigeb had to laugh as well, and then let out a muffled yell of surprise when all seven doors flew open and his friends jumped out.

All eight of them were there. Nigeb later learned that all of them had personally been called by Eranor to come to the Monastery. And all of them had accepted the invitation.

After Nigeb had caught up with the events of the past few days, he finally went into his room, and found his father's diary sitting on a large, comfortable-looking bed.

Chapter 9

The Past and the Future

FIRM WOKE UP THE next day in his large and comfortable bed, inside of his large and bright room. The first thing he did was throw open the windows to let in a gentile breeze. The sun was just rising over the distant hills, and the morning was brilliant.

Firm had already explored the room. He and Thon had been at the Monastery for several days. They were one of the first to arrive with Eranor, and Firm had greatly enjoyed everything the Monastery had to offer. Thon, however, wasn't as happy as he should have been at trading Ullantown for a large city. He was still suspicious about everything and made it painfully clear.

Firm was sold, though. He loved absolutely every single thing, at least for now, and was feeling happy about all eight of them finally being there.

That morning he threw on his clothes and went exploring along the hallways. He was so wound up that he forgot about breakfast and then got lost, making him even more late.

He didn't mind, however. And he was pleased to find that he wasn't last, as Oser had just arrived at the dining room moments before and Nigeb was nowhere to be seen. The rest of the flens were there, however. Thon nonetheless made his presence well known by yawning loudly after finishing his breakfast, and then making a racket of putting away his dishes and utensils.

Nigeb didn't show up at breakfast at all. Later, Firm saw him wandering along the old hallways dimly lit by the morning sun. Firm called out to him and even waved to get his attention but all that provoked was a slight turn of his friend's head and a growled reply. Nigeb seemed preoccupied with some small, tattered book and was taking great interest in the portraits hanging along the hallway, so Firm decided to leave him alone.

Eranor was nowhere to be seen, which disappointed Firm: he really had wanted to talk to him. He wondered what the deal was with Eranor disappearing all the time, but Levi assured him that they would see Dominum's son soon, and that he was always there when he needed to be.

Nonetheless, Firm spent the morning exploring every room and hallway with Thon, absolutely fascinated (Firm was fascinated, not Thon).

They walked through libraries and meeting halls (used long ago), looked inside storage rooms and saw several training rooms.

The training rooms were perhaps the most interesting, with different tools and weapons and shields, and many old contraptions, sort of like obstacle courses on which to train on. Gear of all kind hung or stood in neat rows along the walls. Firm took peculiar interest in the ancient swords that stood in stacks, sheathed and tucked safely away. Firm didn't have a sword of his own: only Levi, Athor, and Oser had one. Nigeb too, but he didn't use his much. Kevin and Tenzin had knives, but Thon and Firm carried no weapons.

Firm knew that he was safe at the moment, but their long adventure had proven that the business they were in was dangerous.

Meanwhile, Thon had turned his attention to the training equipment.

The two cousins were startled when Levi walked up from behind and said softly, "You two don't have swords, do you?"

"Never needed one." Thon announced, and started boxing the huge sand-filled bag used for punching in front of him. The bag was several feet in diameter, and about seven feet tall, so that Thon didn't get very far with it.

Levi watched patiently and then turned back to the swords. After carefully studying row after row of hilt and steel, he finally pulled out a long double-edged, blue-steeled sword with a long hilt ended in a knob shaped like a ball of fire.

Handing it to Firm, sheath and all, he said, "It is time you received your noble blade of justice, Firm Arolin."

Firm was taken by surprise. "But how is it yours to give? Aren't these Eranor's swords?"

Levi smiled, "I am sure that he would want you to have it. Just pull it out."

Firm carefully pulled the blade out and almost dropped it. In the bright morning light, the sword shone a fiery blue, and the name *Firm* appeared along the edge.

Firm, still shocked, examined the sword with interest, turning it round and round. Finally, he managed to say, "How?"

Levi laughed quietly. "I guess it was made for you."

"But what if it does this for everyone?" Firm asked.

"Test your theory," Levi replied.

Firm handed the sword to Levi, and it immediately returned to its natural shade. The name *Firm* vanished, and nothing replaced it.

Levi gave it back. "See? It is yours, and there are no other swords like this with your name on it. This is *your* sword, and you are being entrusted with it. Hold it with honor and protect it, and keep it clean of evil."

"I will," Firm answered, sheathing the sword and buckling it onto his belt.

"I suppose there is a sword for me?" Thon asked dryly. As you might remember, he didn't like being left out.

"There is," Levi replied. "But you will have to find it: I believe it is hiding." Then he started laughing uproariously and turned around and left.

Firm stifled a laugh, and Thon grumbled, "I feel a good dose of favoritism."

After that they left and explored farther up the hallways. Thon kept looking in odd rooms and corners and examined every sword he found. Firm wasn't sure if Thon was taking Levi seriously or if he was joking, but his cousin was willing to explore every inch of the Monastery, and that was something Firm didn't take for granted.

The young flens were surprised to find Levi and Nigeb, who were examining something in the hallway. Thon didn't succeed in his search for his sword and was feeling grumpy. Firm, on the other hand, was relieved to finally see someone: he really had been worried about being lost again.

Levi seemed to be showing something to Nigeb, and the younger flen paid great interest. When Firm and Thon walked up, they saw a large lantern resting on a small round table. The lantern had a large brass handle at the top, and a small, peculiar candle in the middle. Instead of being enclosed in glass, as you might see nowadays, the candle was surrounded by a silk fabric, stretched around four upward poles. The silk was thin but was colorfully designed with a map drawn on it.

"Have you ever seen a map like this?" Levi asked the two cousins, pointing at the lantern. Neither was very good with maps in general and they both shook their heads. "I haven't ever seen one, but Nigeb here seems to think he has."

All four of the flens looked at the small, tattered book Nigeb was holding. Nigeb flipped through it and pointed at another similar map. "This is my father's diary. Here he includes many similarly drawn maps. I still don't understand what most of these maps are but there seems to be a connection. Also, in here he talks about the Lantern of Light."

"This is the Lantern of Light." Levi said, pointing at the lantern.

"Seriously? The Lantern of Light? Don't all lanterns have light? " Thon asked.

Firm knew that Thon, like himself, had no idea what the Lantern of Light was, but that hadn't stopped him from pretending to be interested. And also adding a joke.

"The Lantern of Light," repeated Levi, "is an ancient artifact, a symbol of good and of Dominum's light against the darkness of the Hondaloom. The Lantern of Light is said to 'help mortals see clearly what is plainly in front of them.'"

"Is it magic?" Thon asked hopefully, although rather sarcastically in intent.

"No, not quite, but it is a peculiar thing and is best to be kept safe." Levi replied, not losing a beat to Thon's intended sarcasm.

"Which is why I am trying to find the connection I had." Nigeb interjected. "But I believe it is lunchtime, and I would hate to miss it, as I did with breakfast, so let us hurry back."

✳✳✳

The meal was delicious. It was even better than breakfast, Firm thought, and it was obvious that Nigeb had never tasted anything better.

Firm wondered how all that produce had gotten there, and it didn't occur to him that several of the flens might have gone down to Flenvinhum that morning. For now, he just enjoyed the pastries and fruit.

All of the flens were here this time, and they were seated at a large table in a bright, sun-flooded dining room. All of them had spent the morning exploring, and they were seemingly excited about their adventure thus far. Thon was still acting glum and became glummer still when he found that Levi, Athor, and Oser all had swords that flashed with their names. Thon was especially curious about the sword that Nigeb had found, the one that belonged to Yar and had fallen off the South Bridge. Levi had examined the sword but had found nothing interesting in particular, besides the fact that it looked more like an ancient flen sword than a lun sword, and certainly was more beautiful and better crafted than any lun weapon. But Nigeb himself wasn't sure exactly what the sword was, and it was decided that they would wait to ask Eranor.

However, that took longer than expected. Eranor had set everything to their comfort and had given them the full right to anything in the Monastery. But they didn't see him for the next week. Some of the younger flens were impatient, but Levi reminded them that Eranor was the son of Dominum, and that he never stayed in one place for long.

Nonetheless, the flens were greatly relieved and somewhat excited when he finally returned one cold and misty morning. There was a loud bang at the great double doors, and then Eranor walked in, not bothering to wait until they answered. It was, after all, *his* monastery.

The flens all got to the courtyard as fast as they could, but they were then hustled back inside by Eranor.

"It is now that you must listen to me!" he said as he pushed them back in.

He led them to a large room, plainly furnished but otherwise featureless, and had them all sit down. He stood very quietly and solemnly as they got into their places, but his eyes flashed and his face and figure seemed great and regal. He did not give the impression of an old man right then. Then he began.

"I will now give you a summary and explanation of the story that you have become part of. I will also tell you why you have become part of it, and what must happen before it is completed.

"This story, as all stories, finds its beginning in Dominum, who made the beginning of all things. When the world was still a dark void, Dominum created Erandin into it, as well as the sky and the sea. Then there was no evil, and Dominum's presence was in everything. Beings he also created, and one was he who is now called the Hondaloom, though at first he had a different name. The Hondaloom became jealous of Dominum, and wished to be king of Erandin. He fell from the presence of Dominum, and cursed Erandin, and Dominum left the land.

"There is far more to this story, the story of the Beginning of Erandin and of the Fall of Erandin, but the story in its entirety is not necessary here.

"The Hondaloom cursed Erandin, and the Great Chasm split it from the land of Dominum. The chasm was placed there because of the enemy, but it was by the will of my father. For all evil is forever banished from his land, and the Great Chasm is the barrier that keeps it out. But the curse of the Hondaloom is that '*The Great*

Chasm divides all, he who is born of this world shall fall.' All who are born into Erandin are born into the Hondaloom's wrongful rule, and all have become subject to him. None can cross the Great Chasm and go to Dominum's land. And the Hondaloom wants to make all of Erandin his slaves and wishes to engulf the land in darkness. This is the story as it stands."

There was a moment of silence, and then Firm spoke up very quietly.

"If you don't mind me asking, sir, I don't think I fully understand the curse, and the Great Chasm, and why none can go to Dominum's land, especially if they are for Dominum and against the Hondaloom."

"But I think I do." Levi said. "We are in the stronghold of the Hondaloom, so to speak, and we are trapped in it and held as captives, but it is our fault we are here in the first place, because the fathers of men and flens chose to stay in Erandin when first the Hondaloom fell. They were deceived with false hopes, as Eranor would have told us if he gave us the full account of the Fall of Erandin."

"That is quite right," Eranor agreed. "But though none can cross the Great Chasm and all are under the rule of the Hondaloom, not all is lost. Had the Hondaloom had his way, all of Erandin would have been nothing but endless misery and pain and burning fire, but the enemy is not greater than my father, and my father intervened.

"When the Hondaloom first fell to darkness and brought evil to Erandin, my father saw what must happen and willed a prophecy to be spoken. The prophecy foretold of the coming of eight flens, chosen by Dominum himself, and called by Dominum's son. The focal point of history would be at hand, sides would be taken, the Hondaloom would pour out his forces, and the final and deciding battle between Dominum and those with him against the Hondaloom would begin. All that has ever happened has led up to this point, and this point alone."

Somewhere outside a bird called out, and Nigeb was momentarily shaken out of his thinking. The purpose of the world was being told to him by the son of Dominum, and he was filled with an unexplainable feeling of wonder and insight to the great heroes of Old and the vast darkness they fought so bravely. And also that all their deeds and battles would lead up to this point of time, which he had so unexpectedly become a part of.

But all was still and quiet in the room, and Eranor spoke again.

"Some of you have asked me why the enemy has been quiet for so many years, and Athor especially was curious."

"Yes, that is true," Athor answered. "I was surprised at all the trouble we went through to get here, especially the wolves that Nigeb fought."

"Yes," Eranor continued. "It should be known to at least some that the Hondaloom waged war against the three brothers of Old: Non, Don, and Ron, who were mighty heroes and warriors. The Hondaloom could not overcome them, and much of his power he lost when he was defeated. But he was not destroyed or defeated for good, only for a time. And after that, he began exerting his will in subtler ways, and began to prepare for the fulfillment of the prophecy. He has waited for the coming of the eight flens, and for Dominum's son.

"Many have forgotten of his power, but the Hondaloom has been brooding his plan of becoming the sole ruler of Erandin since he fell to evil. All has been quiet, but that is about to change. His power is growing and his armies are gathering. Many luns are loyal to him, and he has other, more evil servants. Already the lands of Holoom are fully under his control, and few dare go near there. The North is becoming more dangerous, too. Wild animals and savage beasts are returning to those lands and have been roaming freely. But the place to which the Hondaloom has most set his eyes on is the Realm of Non, the lands to the south of Holoom. All this is far away from Flenvinhum, but news are coming even to here of the continuous run-on attacks that the enemy is making on that great land of men.

"But the problem that you are most faced with, my flens, is not only the Great Chasm but that you cannot fight or even resist the Hondaloom, yet. For the Hondaloom is not mortal or made of flesh and bones, but is a spirit of great power. And so the efforts of weapons like metal swords and iron spears have no effect on him and his strongest servants.

"But now I come to the point of what you must do next, now that you have come to Flenvinhum. My flens, you must become Azoons, the warriors of Old, and the warriors of Dominum and his son. The Azoons were the first to side with my father against the Hondaloom, and there are none of their like in the world today. For only Azoons can know the secret to the Armor of Light. I am sure that you have never heard of this armor, but know that only through it may a mortal have the power to fight a spirit like that of the Hondaloom."

Eranor stopped and surveyed the room, looking intently at each and every flen, as if he could read their thoughts, which, no doubt, he could. "Tomorrow we shall continue."

After that, all the flens returned to whatever they had been doing, each thinking his own thoughts.

Chapter 10

The Map of Azoons

NIGEB HAD FELT A large weight lifted from his shoulders after he met Eranor. He had been anxious about where his adventure was going, and he had risked his life several times in trying to get to Flenvinhum. And he hadn't even known what was awaiting him. Now he knew about his parents and had become very interested in what Eranor had to offer. Dominum's son had changed his life.

As Nigeb thought these thoughts, he was slowly shining his sword with a rag. It was the same sword he had received at the South Bridge. "Received" was debatable, as some might say that it wasn't given to him willingly. But it looked fabulous in all its glimmering light and glory. It was a sword of medium length, with small features, and no doubt it was small in Yar's filthy hands. But it was a sword to behold, and Nigeb wondered where it could have been made.

One thing he noticed, however, was that the handle was undoubtably longer than that of most swords. There was a faint spiral design that ran from the top of the handle to the bottom, and it ended in a large, blue knob.

At first, he paid little attention to it, and mostly concentrated on pretending to battle invisible opponents, practicing parries and thrusts, defensive and offensive positions. He became quite comfortable with the feel and balance of the sword, and often enjoyed fantasizing all the adventures he would have with it. Now that he could use it better, he wished that he could use it more often in real situations. Little did he know that war is a terrible thing.

As Nigeb shined his sword, he noticed a curious thing. The handle twisted a little if a certain amount of strength were applied. It unscrewed more and more as he twisted it. He was unsure of himself—after all, was the handle meant to unscrew? And if so, what could possibly be inside?

After several minutes of twisting the top of the handle, the blue knob suddenly fell off and landed with a *thud* on the floor.

Nigeb stooped down, picked it up, and then turned his attention to the rest of the sword. There was a hollow in the handle, and the end of a rolled up piece of parchment poked out. Nigeb slowly, almost cautiously, pulled it out.

What he found in his hand was a rolled up map! It was well-preserved and still had good color, but the thing that Nigeb noticed right away were the words written on the bottom left corner: *We flens were tasked with the assignment of serving good and protecting Erandin from evil, of living good and honest lives.*

The same words as on his father's map!

Nigeb immediately dug up the satchel with his father's map from one of his bags to compare the two.

It was one whole map! His father's map was the top half, and the map from the sword was the bottom half. The map made more sense now; there was an island surrounded by the Sea of Erandin, and a structure marked *Temple of Truth* near the middle.

But what baffled Nigeb the most was the fact that half of his father's map was hidden in a sword that had been in the possession of the captain of the luns! What was the meaning of it all? Eranor had talked of his father's affairs in mapmaking and actively fighting the Hondaloom, but how could all of this be happening? Whatever it was, he now had the full map and it seemed to be quite important. Nigeb decided that it was time Eranor saw it.

***

"It was in the sword." Nigeb said.

Eranor had been inspecting both halves of the map along with the sword. He had seemed especially interested in the noble blade and had held it for a while. But to Nigeb it seemed that Dominum's son already knew what it was—and no doubt he did.

Eranor handed the sword back to Nigeb. "You were right in your assumption, for this is one of your father's maps."

But Nigeb didn't quite hear what Eranor said, because the sword dimly lit up. It then brightened to the color of a dying fire, and the name *Nigeb* flashed along the blade. As can be expected, Nigeb was flabbergasted; he knew nothing of the other blades of similar type, the ones that several of his friends possessed, and this was something he had never seen before.

Once Nigeb recovered from his initial shock, Eranor continued. "This sword, my young friend, belonged to your father. It was lost to the luns of Holoom when your father perished, and its secret was also forgotten. Until now."

Nigeb nodded, thinking it through. He had read through most of his father's diary and did recall him speaking of such a sword. But now his mind wandered through the diary's pages, the ones that talked about all the times his father escaped or was rescued in strange, unusual, and unexplainable ways.

"This was your doing." Nigeb finally said. Eranor waited to hear what else he had to say. "You not only cut the South Bridge so that we could escape, but you made it so that I fell and found the sword, and you somehow managed to land the sword on that ledge in the first place, despite it falling out of Yar's hands somewhere in the middle of the bridge! The Hondaloom and the luns meant our meeting for evil, but you reversed the effects into something that had to happen!"

Eranor laughed and said, "You are quick to put things together."

"The only thing that remains to be made clear is *what* the map is pointing to. I already suspected from the beginning that this map was important, and I see that I am right."

"You are very right, my friend, once again." Eranor replied. "But before I explain this, I need all of you here."

**

The flens gathered this time in the outside courtyard. They made themselves comfortable, and perked up their ears. They could sense that something important was coming. Thon was grumbling, as he still hadn't found his sword, and certainly would have felt worse had he found out about Nigeb's.

Eranor hushed everybody up, and then started. "I have already talked to you about becoming Azoons, and now I shall continue with that."

He motioned for Nigeb to come up, and then put a hand on his shoulder. "As you all must already know, Nigeb had found a sword, a very peculiar and interesting sword that had been in the possession of a lun."

He took the sword from Nigeb, held it for everybody to see, and then revealed the compartment with the complete map inside. Several of the flens got up to have a better look.

Eranor beckoned the rest. "Come closer, come closer, get a good view, this map is very important."

After all the flens had looked and were standing in a tight circle, Eranor continued.

"This map was made by Nigeb's father, Nilleb. Nilleb Fortrute was his full name."

To the many questions, he answered, "Nigeb can tell you all about it and him after I'm through. Now, this map, called the Map of Azoons, will show you where you can learn the secret of the Armor of Light. The *Temple of Truth* is clearly marked here, that should be easy enough to remember. The *Temple of Truth* is where you must go, there you will find the secret to the Armor of Light.

"However, you are not Azoons yet. You have journeyed across a vast distance in answer to my summons and have all come to the Monastery, but that is only the beginning. To become Azoons, you must complete this journey. And if you truly wish to do so, then you will find the Temple of Truth and you will learn the secret to the Armor of Light. But you will go without me."

Murmured protests rose up but Eranor quieted them.

"I will go now to confer with my father, and then I have other business. You aren't, after all, the only ones who have sided with me against the Hondaloom. There are others, and they are in urgent need of my aid."

With that, he turned around and went back into the Monastery. The flens knew that he would leave soon and they troubled him no more but turned to Levi. He was their leader in Eranor's absence.

The first thing that Levi did was hand out three very special swords to Kevin, Tenzin, and Thon. Thon was most excited on receiving his very own sword, a sword that flashed his name every time he held it or thrust it. After the three flens had had time to gaze at their weapons, Levi finally spoke. "Eranor gave me these for you as protection from evil but also as a gift."

He surveyed the seven flens. "What have you chosen? My life is now to tell of Eranor's power over the Hondaloom."

Athor clasped Levi's shoulder. "You don't think I would have come all this way just to go back, do you? It'll take more than one fight to scare me."

Levi smiled and said, "If I remember correctly, there have been two fights so far."

Oser drew his sword, and his name flashed across it. "I am with Dominum and his son."

"So am I." Kevin said.

"As am I." Tenzin remarked.

Firm spoke up. "I confess, I wasn't sure of where all of this was going when I first met Eranor but I knew it was something to behold. So tell me why I would turn back now?"

Nigeb looked at Thon. Thon half-whispered, half-growled, "I'll wait until we learn the secret to the Armor of Light, but I will go with you."

Then Nigeb said, "I certainly could not turn back now, now that I have learned of the evil Hondaloom, and of the hope that

Eranor has given us in defeating him and freeing us from the curse we are under. I am with Dominum and his son until the end."

"Eranor certainly knew what he was doing when he chose the eight of us." Levi said. "We are now in this together. Now, let's have a closer look at that map."

***

After sewing the map together, the flens spent hours brooding over it. Their problem was not knowing exactly where the island on the map was. There were several islands off of Erandin's coastline, and visiting all of them was out of the question. Their hope was to try and locate the island and then to find the Temple of Truth using the map. But little was known about the islands in the Sea of Erandin, not to mention the Temple of Truth. Until the flens singled out the island, there was nothing else to do.

The Monastery proved to be an excellent study place with many books and charts of just about everything. But it would be impossible to go through everything down to the very word. They plowed through manuscript after manuscript, reading and going over anything that had to do with islands, temples, the Armor of Light, and Azoons. But they got no closer to finding the island, although they learned a good deal of information on topics varying from how to build castles to surviving in the wild off of strange substances.

Thon had never learned this much information in one go before, and after a little while he found it necessary to lie down in bed and eat honey on bread.

The others were also getting frustrated by then and were constantly getting lost in the long, winding hallways.

"Eranor knew what he was talking about when he said that this would be hard!" Athor mumbled under his breath as the sun began to set. "But who would believe that we would get stuck right at the beginning? If we're busting ourselves over this now, how will we fare when real danger comes? Being an Azoon would certainly be easier if it meant that Eranor would give us all the answers while we pretended that we knew what was happening. I'm sure he knows exactly what island we need to go to and I'm sure he could take us there in an instant if he needed to!"

"Take heart, dear friend, the battle is far from over." Levi answered his old friend. "Hardships bring out character, and character brings out hope, and hope is one of the best things in a world that we do not fully understand. Eranor will help us yet, be sure of that!"

But it is not easy to see the good in life when hardship is upon you, and the flens soon felt the despair of the matter. After not being able to find any references or pointers on what island the Temple of Truth was located at, they turned to examining the Map of Azoons itself.

"It's a magical map, pointing to a magical temple, on a magical island!" Thon grumbled. He had been forced to get up and was not at all happy about it. "Clearly this map has something to do with magic, and clearly it will only work properly if magic is applied to it!"

The other flens looked at him, impressed. Most of them weren't quite sure that the map was entirely magical, but it had them thinking in the right direction. But not much credit should be given to Thon. After all, he had had plenty of time to think it over while lying in bed.

"If it is truly magic," Levi said slowly, "then there should be something we could use to 'reveal' what we're looking for."

"Like a magic wand?" Athor asked.

"Maybe not a wand, but something like a wand." Nigeb said excitedly. "Maybe there's a certain tool we could use, something that would make everything clear."

Suddenly, his eyes lit up and he hastily pulled his father's diary out. "Levi, do you remember what you said about the Lantern of Light?"

Levi thought back. "Yes, there is an old saying that the Lantern of Light *helps mortals see clearly what is plainly in front of them*. But how does that help?"

Nigeb was thinking it through. "Athor said that Eranor would have been able to tell us how to find the island. But Eranor isn't a mortal: he's the son of Dominum. We, on the other hand, are mortals, so the saying is talking about us!"

"Are you implying that we'll die before we find this island?" Thon scoffed.

"No, no," Nigeb hurriedly answered. "The explanation said that mortals like us will be able to see clearly what is plainly in front of us. This map is plainly in front of us but we don't see clearly."

Levi was catching on. "So we need to use the Lantern of Light to help us see it clearly. The only question is what to see clearly?"

"There's only one way to find out." Nigeb announced.

"Kevin," Levi said. "You're the fastest of us all. Go and fetch the Lantern of Light, will you?"

Kevin obeyed and quickly got the lantern. The flens lit it and began. At first, no one was quite sure what to do.

"Wait! Wait!" Oser shouted. "Give it to me."

As soon as the lantern was handed over to him, he said, "There might be magic involved alright, but what if the answer is more logical than we think? After all, the lantern will help us see *clearly* what is *plainly in front of us.*"

With these words, Oser took the Lantern of Light and held it in front of the map.

Nothing happened.

Undaunted, he lifted the map and then held the lantern in front of it. But even if something was there, it could not be seen due to the reflection of light.

Finally, Oser lifted the Lantern of Light over the map and put it *behind* the map.

Instantly, all the flens could see the large, bold letters now visible from the light shining through the map. The light dimmed all else on the map and from the now transparent inside the words *SafeHaven* could be read.

"SafeHaven!" Levi exclaimed. "The lantern worked!"

"What could it mean?" Tenzin asked.

"Most likely it's the name of the island that we need." Oser said, closely examining the map without lowering the lantern. He then removed the lantern and the words disappeared. "It's all logic, after all."

"Do you suppose the words would not show had we used another source of light?" Firm asked curiously.

"No time for that now," Levi said. "First priority is finding more information on 'SafeHaven.' Somebody, go fetch a geography atlas."

After Kevin returned with the atlas (he was usually the errand boy), the flens immediately searched through the island section, and eventually they indeed found what they were looking for: the island of SafeHaven, located off of the southwestern coast of Erandin, and perhaps the largest island of them all.

But despite its size, next to nothing was known about it, due to the fact of it being the "forbidden island," where no one dared to go. Something powerful was involved with it, something that frightened explorers and sea-goers.

But this was the island that the flens needed.

Levi smiled a grim smile. "I hope that you brought your sailing gear."

Chapter 11

Seasick

THE FLENS HAD LEFT the next morning, with little preparations or training. They had packed over night, bringing any
essential gear and tools. Now, several days journey by horse later,
they had managed to buy a boat—a large, well constructed, and
beautifully painted sailboat—and were loading it.

Outside of his recent adventures, Nigeb had no experience
at sailing boats or finding hidden temples or battling luns or any
other possible dangers that they might meet.

But (surprise, surprise) the other flens, except for Thon and
Firm, had either done a little bit of everything or a lot of several
things. Most of them knew the specifics of sailing, and Tenzin had
once steered a boat across the Centered Lake. Because of this, they
felt pretty confident of their chances.

But for Nigeb, it was hard to feel safe about something that
was presumably very unsafe.

And from Firm's appearance, he was thinking the same thing.
Thon didn't look very well either. The sea was his enemy, and the
waves were looking very ugly.

After everything was ready and Thon had more or less
convinced himself to step on board, the flens set sail and left the
harbor.

The flens had traveled directly west from the Monastery, until they reached a small harbor with many a sailboat anchored there. They had sold their horses and bought a boat without any inconveniences, but they were now completely out of money.

Not that it mattered; after all, they would be sailing to Safe-Haven, and then they would search for a temple on a deserted island. They would have to rely on themselves and only on themselves. At least, this is what most of the flens thought.

As the flens sailed on through the day, the sea stayed calm and quiet, the waves smoothly lapping against the hull of the boat in a steady rhythm. The wind was strong and blew in the desired direction—south. It was an enjoyable sort of weather, and it was fairly warm.

The flens did fine for most of that day, taking turns at steering and doing various tasks around the deck, while the others lazily reclined below the deck or on it, trying to calm themselves before the trouble began. Nigeb felt okay at being at sea, but he certainly didn't like the idea of having to run into a storm with nothing but water around. The others seemed more calm, all except for Thon, happy and carefree, joke-cracking, witty fella Thon, who was terrified of the sea and spent most of his time in the below deck with a terrible case of seasickness.

But the trouble began at the end of the day, when the clouds darkened and rain began to fall. The power and strength of the waves intensified, and the wind sped up. The flens were now far from shore, going at a south course directly for the island of Safe-Haven, and would arrive in several hours, provided that all went well.

But now it seemed that a storm was possible. Everyone assembled at the top deck, except for Thon, and began making the necessary preparations. The sails were lowered, and everything was moved below deck or tied securely to the main deck.

No sooner had they done this than a storm, which had been brewing on the horizon, fell upon them in a great fury and intensity. Waves broke upon the sailboat and the wind lashed violently at the hull and all the passengers. Several times the flens were nearly swept away by an especially large wave as they tried to steady the boat. Tying themselves to the mast and each other helped keep them from going overboard, but did little to sooth them as the sailboat was thrown from side to side.

The sky was black with clouds and was often lit up with lightning. It was also raining hard now, and began hailing at one point on top of everything. There was nothing in sight save for darkness and water.

Nigeb was thrown here and there, and as he focused on staying alive, he couldn't help but remember Thon, who must be retching and scared half to death at that very moment.

Nigeb had been leaning against the railing when he saw a large black shape looming not to far to the right. As it drew nearer, it became obvious that it was a ship, much larger than that of the flens. And it was heading right for them.

At first, Nigeb assumed it must be some coast guard or friendly soul, coming to rescue them. But as the flens began trying to change their course to the direction of the large ship, lightning illuminated the sky, revealing the black sails atop the mast of the ship and the huge dragon's head at the helm.

These weren't rescuers: they were pirates, or worse, luns!

"Mayday! Mayday!" Nigeb exclaimed. "Those are pirates!"

Levi could see that right away. "Change course! Lighten the load! Prepare for attack! Arm yourselves!"

Several flens just drew their swords, their names flashing across the blades, when the pirates were alongside them, and boarding their sailboat.

There were many of them, at least twenty. They were big and powerful, and yelled in a strange language. They were armed with swords and axes, and several carried huge bows with deadly arrows. They had painted faces, and were most unpleasant.

"Luns!" Nigeb exclaimed as he came face to face with none other than Yar, the luns' general.

The brute aimed a powerful blow at Nigeb with his club. The flen had just enough time to bring out his own sword and parry the blow, but the force of it knocked him flat on his back.

Nigeb had enough time to see Athor come out of nowhere and throw himself at the large lun, forcing him back with his sword, when the boat lurched heavily to the side, and all passengers, invited or uninvited, rolled over in one direction.

Nigeb only managed to stop moving when he thudded against the railing. Instantly, he seized a shield, and he and the nearest lun faced off. They exchanged blows and fought viciously, Nigeb feeling a strength he never had before. Indeed, this was the first battle that he participated in. After all, the fight at the South Bridge was something he was hardly a part of.

The luns were increasing in numbers. But the flens fought valiantly, and kept them at bay to an extent. But seven (remember that Thon wasn't there) against twenty-seven can hardly be called even, though some (but not all) of the flens were more than a match for several luns.

Nigeb had just heaved up his shield in time to stop a sword thrust, when the boat forcefully leaned to the side again, this time in the opposite direction of the luns' ship.

"Land ho!" Oser cried from the sailboat's helm. He was standing behind the wheel, and turning it sharply in the direction of a large, dark spot on the horizon.

The island! The island of SafeHaven!

The flens' sailboat broke away from their enemies' ship, and set their course for the island.

Half of the luns had already retreated. The others, seeing their ship start to slip away and also how dangerously low their numbers were falling, retreated immediately by jumping down into a rowboat and vigorously rowing back to their vessel.

The flens fought their way towards the island, but although they were now free from the luns' pursuit, they were failing miserably against the ferocious storm.

The island seemed to draw nearer, and then it almost vanished completely from sight as the flens were thrown back and their sailboat hit by wave after wave in the endless darkness, as if the world had vanished completely.

Nigeb felt his head spinning in circles when he caught a glimpse of Thon, struggling up the stairs that led onto the deck. His body swayed from side to side, and he had to stop every several moments to clutch his stomach. In fact, had Nigeb not felt exactly the same way, he may have remarked that Thon looked very different from his usual jolly self.

Instead, he staggered over to where Thon was, and helped steady him and keep him from falling, being more stable-footed than his friend.

But Thon shrugged him off and stumbled over to the railing, which he gripped so tightly that his knuckles became white. He stared into the roaring waves for some time, while the other flens, unaware of his presence, continued with their navigation.

All at once, Thon shouted out to the waves, "I am not afraid! I am not afraid! You don't scare me anymore! I am not afraid!"

A streak of lightning lit the sky, cutting through the very storm, as if it were mustering its last strength. The lightning pierced through the storm, melting it all away. The waves ceased their uproar all at once, and the wind died down. All was quiet again; the lun's ship was out of sight.

"What was that!?" Athor roared from the helm.

Thon remained at the railing, clutching it as if the storm was still raging around him. He kept staring into the water, until Nigeb walked up to him and put a hand on his shoulder.

"Tell me," he asked his friend, "did the calming of the storm come from you?"

"Not as much from me as from the power behind Eranor." Thon answered. He straightened up again and seemed to relax, but he still had a death grip on the railing.

The other flens, still getting used to the idea that the storm and danger was over, started moving around the deck, seeing if they were all in one piece. Eventually, though, they started gathering around Nigeb and Thon, curious to know what had happened.

"Has anyone here seen something like that before?" Oser asked. "Has anyone seen a storm go from raging at full force to nothing whatsoever?"

"I'm assuming you have an explanation, Thon?" Nigeb asked.

Thon nodded. "I do. You all probably saw how scared I was. Well, I was petrified. Up until now, I had never fully trusted Eranor. I didn't have anything personally against him, but while I believed that Dominum existed—how else would our world have come into being?—I thought that Eranor was a fake. It didn't occur to me that he could very possibly be Dominum's son, and I doubted him from the beginning.

"Well, when I first met him, I started having doubts about my doubts. I am a fan of those stories where characters double-cross and triple-cross and the good guy turns out to be the bad guy or vice versa. And it was easy to think that Eranor wasn't who he said he was, and that he was really against Dominum, the real king of Erandin.

"But these thoughts came into my head when I still hadn't met him. However, it was impossible to deny that he was who he said he was when I met him. There is something about him that speaks the absolute truth and that triumphs over the darkness. This may or may not convince someone who has to take my word for it, but I am sure that they will be convinced when they meet Dominum's son for real.

"But even after I was convinced that he was in fact Dominum's son, I still wasn't ready to follow him, something that all of you have already done. You see, I thought to myself, 'Well, I lived fine up until now, and I certainly don't need Eranor for anything right now, either.'

"But I then decided to come along with you on this journey to SafeHaven. Partly, I still wanted to know more about Eranor, but on the other hand, I wanted to see just how far I could get without him.

"I confess, I failed the second we started our sea voyage. I have never been on a boat before, and never at sea like this. I fell to a severe illness immediately. Then, the storm overtook us, and I was about ready to pass out. But I was too scared to even do that. I realized that I could do nothing against a storm of that power. I didn't even have the power to calm and rid myself of the agony I was experiencing. I desperately needed someone who was strong enough to do for me what I couldn't do on my own. Well, Dominum created Erandin, didn't he? He created this world when nothing yet existed here. I thought of Eranor, of how he would have been able to help us, had he been here. But you know what? He *was* here!

"As I wished for Eranor's presence, I was suddenly aware that I was completely engulfed in darkness. Suddenly, as if descending an invisible staircase from the ceiling of my room, a large, brilliantly shining figure appeared. Another similar figure, but more human like, stood to his right. Dominum and Eranor it was, just don't ask me how I knew, because I knew that it couldn't be anyone else, with the same sureness that the sun will rise tomorrow morning. They both stood shining like the sun in all its glory. They were both fully clad in burning armor and mail, with swords at their sides: the Armor of Light. And Dominum held the key to the Armor of Light. Then the room exploded into a blinding flash of light, as if the sun had come in. Dominum, his son, and the key merged into a brilliant bolt of light, flooding out all the darkness and consuming the entire room. They were One, and they completely overpowered the darkness.

"They were in my room, they had been standing there! My doubts were removed; I knew that Dominum was the true King of Erandin, and that Eranor had been sent to our aid, because on our own we would get nowhere, not especially on this journey. And I knew that Dominum's son was stronger than a storm. I was no longer afraid, and the storm had nothing to hold over my head. It left."

It was quiet as the flens processed what they had heard.

"Wow," Nigeb finally said. "How long did it take you to think through all that? No wonder you were sick all the time."

"That is a one-of-a-kind confession, Thon." Kevin confirmed. "I had no idea that this was all going through your mind."

"Firm is probably getting a kick out of this." Thon said. "He was always embarrassed with my behavior."

He looked around. "Firm? Are you here, Firm?"

The flens all began looking around and counting themselves. There were seven of them in all.

"Where's Firm?" Levi asked. "I just saw him somewhere here." Then he picked something up.

It was a sword with blue steel. Firm's sword.

"Where has he gone?" Thon asked, frantically.

"He is on that island," Levi said, pointing at SafeHaven, now steadily becoming larger.

The flens immediately manned the sailboat, let down the sails, and set in the direction of the island, now a large green shape on the horizon. And far ahead, just off the island's coastline, was a large black ship.

The luns' ship.

Chapter 12

The Fox and the Hounds

THE FLENS NOW NEARED the island.

It was a large island, green with forests, but topped off with gray looming mountains. The water became clear and tropical, with the occasional stingray or seal swimming by. The island had a long beach, white with sand, but beyond that were dense tropics.

According to Nigeb's father's map, there was a valley down the middle of SafeHaven, lined with mountains on either side. The Temple of Truth was located at the end of that valley, but unless there were direction signs, things promised to be difficult.

But the flens were thinking of a different type of difficulty. Firm was missing—there was no doubt that the luns had taken him captive—and now the flens had to find him first, hopefully unharmed, before they could do anything else.

The fates of good and evil were certainly intertwined at this hour. The luns' ship had been seen landing on a wide strip of beach, and while this meant that the flens would certainly have difficulties in reaching the Temple of Truth without a fight, it also meant that Firm was in the reach of saving.

The flens had quietly sailed partly around the island and away from the luns. Although they doubted that they had gone by unseen, at least there would be no unpleasant surprises when they landed.

Upon finding a small, secluded bay, the flens anchored and lowered a rowboat.

They had anchored far away from where they had seen the luns, and their hope was that the sailboat would remain untouched at their return. But their own lives being at stake worried them more than their sailboat's safety.

They rowed to the white beach, where they pulled their rowboat into some vegetation, so concealing it from sight. After that, the seven flens took up any bags that they had brought with them, double-checked their provisions and arms, and lumbered into the tropical vegetation. Nigeb and Levi went at the front of the line, wielding compasses and the Map of Azoons.

They trekked through the jungle all morning. Their going was quiet and quick, and they only stopped once, for no more than half an hour, in order to eat and refill their bottles.

It was hot. The summer sun was hidden from their view above the jungle tree tops, but the humidity was high, and the bugs swarmed in huge clouds. Several times, the group spotted different animals, but most were small, although not entirely harmless.

The flens had decided on their course of action ahead of time. They would first find the luns, and then somehow free Firm (but how was still to be discussed). Then they would go in search of the Temple of Truth. They would need to receive the secret of the Armor of Light, and then leave. But it was clear that certain obstacles may be involved (mostly the luns).

As they began to approach the side of the island where the luns had been seen landing, the flens began discussing their plan to free Firm.

They first sent Kevin ahead in order to find out exactly where the luns were, and then Levi started. "We are obviously not a match for all the luns combined, especially considering that there could be more than we first saw. If Firm is still out of harm's way, by the will of Dominum, then he will most likely be guarded and imprisoned. The question is how to free Firm and escape without the luns following us."

The question was not left hanging, and Athor jumped in immediately.

"The luns know that we are on the island," he pointed out. "So it would be preposterous to assume we won't have trouble. So instead of having the trouble of them chasing us as we free Firm *and* as we search for the Temple of Truth, I say that we split in half. Then half of us will go rescue Firm, giving those luns all the trouble they want, while the other half takes advantage of the luns' preoccupation and finds the Temple of Truth."

But Levi immediately pointed out the flaws in Athor's plan.

"Athor, remember that freeing Firm isn't our only top priority, forgive me, Thon, for my manner of speaking. We must remember that we came here to receive the secret of the Armor of Light. All of us must receive it, so splitting in half is pointless."

"But wait," Oser interjected. "Maybe Athor is onto something regarding the point where he talked about the luns' preoccupation."

"I knew I was onto *something*." Athor mumbled, out of hearing range.

Oser continued. "Levi is right about us having to stay together, but what if we could cause a diversion, and then *one* of us, in order to stay undetected, would make his way to where Firm is, and free him. Then, while the luns are still preoccupied, all eight of us could quickly disappear off the scene."

Kevin arrived at that moment, clearly out of breath, but looking triumphant. "I'll bet you ten to one that none of you could have run that fast."

"We believe you," Thon said. "Where is Firm?"

"Okay," Kevin began. "The luns' camp is far closer than we thought. They are camping on the beach, near their ship. They have few sentries, so few that I was able to get in close, but otherwise, their camp is crawling with luns, no less than thirty. Obviously, there is more than we first thought. They have lots of tents, and look like they're preparing for battle."

"The plot thickens," Athor murmured.

"Did you see Firm at all?" Nigeb asked. He was more worried about his friend than some of the other flens.

"Yes," Kevin excitedly confirmed. "He is in a small, wooden cage, suspended in the middle of the camp on a tree, but otherwise he seems unharmed. I tried to make myself seen to him, but those sentries were actually getting close, and I had to make a run for it."

"That certainly changes things," Levi said.

"One more thing," Kevin added. "There is a large river, part of which flows parallel to the camp at some distance. It has a strong current, but isn't violent and doesn't have any waves. Above all, it goes in the direction of the valley. So we could possibly use it for means of transportation."

"Not transportation," Oser said with a faraway look. "We could use it for escape."

Kevin looked at him with a surprised expression. "Excuse me?"

Oser voiced his theory. "I have it! I know how we can rescue Firm! The six of you will cause a diversion, preferably something that will get the luns to leave their camp. I will go into the camp alone, and break Firm out of there. By then, you six will have already escaped to the river. You will then have several minutes to make a raft or something of that sort, so that when Firm and I arrive, we can make a quick escape."

"That's your masterplan?" Athor asked, incredulous. "Sorry buddy, but that may not cut it."

The flens then heard a loud bang, like something heavy had been dropped or a smith hammer had been struck. They immediately hunkered down and froze. The vegetation hid them well.

"We're here," Kevin announced.

"You think you could have given us a heads-up earlier?" Athor growled.

"Now what?" Nigeb asked. He knew this was a bad time to get into an argument.

"We have no other choice," Levi said. "We'll have to go with Oser's plan."

"You say that like it is a bad thing," Oser mumbled.

"Go!"

Oser grabbed Firm's sword and quickly vanished amid the foliage as he began creeping towards the luns' camp.

"We need a diversion," Tenzin said.

"I think I have an idea," Thon suddenly said.

The flens followed Thon's lead as he slowly made his way down the hill towards the most inland part of the luns' camp. They moved slowly, hunching down in the vegetation or even crawling through it, carefully listening for any sound that might announce the presence of a lun. Stealthily, they made their way around the camp, and came to a rest in a thicket of trees several hundred yards away.

Thon began to rummage through any bags that the flens had brought, occasionally taking various items out. When he began pulling out little containers and bowls, he began explaining to the rest of the flens. "These are explosives. Seeing the scare that Eranor had given the luns at the South Bridge gave me an idea. You see, if we could light up the sky with fireworks, then we might just be able to get their attention without them actually seeing us. We would then be able to slip away to the river while they are racing to fight the unknown enemy."

"How are you going to make fireworks?" Athor asked, once again incredulous. He was usually the one with the crazy plans and ideas, and was simply dumbstruck.

"Could all of you gather some firewood and especially some dried up fruits or plants? And one of you is going to need to keep watch." Thon said, and then settled down to working on his ingredients.

***

Oser had already quietly maneuvered his way into the outskirts of the luns' camp. It was a large camp, mostly made of tents, but there were several large fire pits and a few quickly made simple structures. There was certainly more of the enemy than Oser had remembered seeing, and they were preparing. Preparing for battle was his best guess, but what battle? Against eight flens? There would undoubtedly be a large amount of unforeseen events in store.

Oser was currently crouching behind a large weapon stand, and carefully getting an idea of his surroundings. He had already spotted Firm, unharmed, but completely out of options for escape. There was no way for either one of them to do anything without the luns spotting them first.

The other flens would have to dream up a truly ingenious idea.

Oser darted from his hiding place and concealed himself behind a tent. He was confident in his own expertise.

He listened for any noise of possible luns nearby, but this part of camp was quiet.

Oser took a chance and quickly darted into the tent.

No one was there, but he knew that he wouldn't be able to stay in there forever. Some clothing and other luns' belongings were thrown on the floor. Oser considered wearing a disguise, but he knew that he wouldn't even come close to looking like a lun. Only Athor had any chance of passing as a lun, and only because of his size; he would still be unable to talk with the same voice and accent as a true lun, and would have to hide his face.

But thinking of when his accomplices would finally get that diversion working gave him an idea. A cunningly appropriate idea, something that would work as a double distraction and take advantage of the luns' dim minds.

Oser stealthily left the tent and made his way behind several large plants, positioning himself several dozen feet behind Firm's suspended cage. He then took out his small pocketknife, the one engraved *Oser*, took careful aim, and whipped it through the air. It struck one of the wooden bars that made up Firm's cage with a thud. Oser quickly ducked, but when he looked up he saw Firm pulling it out, and carefully looking out for any luns.

Once he was satisfied that Firm had begun cutting away at the ropes that held the cage's door shut, Oser stealthily made his way back to the empty tent.

***

Firm had pulled the knife out, although with some difficulties. He immediately saw the name *Oser* written on the handle, and realized that he was in the middle of a rescue mission!

How excited he was!

He had spent the entire day feeling like a failure, stuck in captivity, with no way to know whether or not his friends would come through for him.

Now he acted fast, sawing through the ropes that bound the small door shut, watching out for any luns. He was confident that his friends had a plan, but what plan exactly was still unknown. For now, he carefully worked on freeing himself, trusting that everything was under control.

Just as he finished sawing through the main rope, a deafening sound demolished the quiet atmosphere of the island, and blinding flashes of light rocketed through the sky, before exploding high above the camp.

At that instance, a large tent at the edge of the beach caught fire, and was instantly consumed. Firm just glimpsed Oser slinking speedily away as half of the luns immediately ran either in the direction of the tent or the direction of the rockets. The other half scattered, totally petrified.

Firm was suddenly aware that Oser had appeared beside him and was now determinedly shaking the cage.

Firm aimed a powerful kick at the door and tumbled out of the cage.

Oser immediately dragged him to his feet, took his knife back, and dashed toward the jungle. Firm was right at his heels.

Shouts told them that they had been spotted, but they were instantly gone, disappearing from sight.

Oser ran hard through the vegetation and foliage, dodging obstacles. Firm kept up admirably, but was starting to doubt that Oser knew where he was going, especially when they passed the same large stump twice, having to double back due to obstacles that they couldn't pass.

Oser finally burst out onto a large bank with a river down below. The sounds of pursuit were close behind, much closer than what Firm was comfortable with.

The rest of the flens were on the bank, having pulled several logs and tree trunks out onto it. They looked very stressed.

"What happened!" Athor yelled. "They're right behind you."

"I freed Firm, didn't I?" Oser answered.

"How . . . did . . . you . . . manage . . . everything?" Firm gasped.

"No time for that," Levi announced. "How are we going to make our escape? We are the fox, and the hounds are nearly upon us."

Nigeb, being of perhaps better hearing than his friends, suddenly heard the signs of very near pursuit. They had no time left.

As the flens began to move the logs and descend down the steep bank, Nigeb suddenly gave a huge heave, toppling the whole set of logs down into the water, as well as some indignant flens.

Just as he did, a dozen luns spilled out of the jungle, howling and yelling.

The flens were all now in the water, grabbing onto logs and gaining control over the situation. Nigeb, however, was still on the bank, and with nothing else left to do, he flung himself down into the river.

It was a great leap. It cleared the bank and shallow edge of the river, and escaped the luns, but it was somewhat desperate, and Nigeb, still being amateur at this type of thing, completely missed the broad log that he had been aiming for and splashed into the water.

He immediately went under, the river being full of various objects, and found that the current was terribly strong, something that Kevin had warned of.

Athor's strong hand, bless him, then hauled him up out of the water and onto the large tree trunk that he was on himself.

The luns were now running along the bank, relentlessly following their escaping enemies. More of them had appeared, and some had begun jumping into the river.

The flens were fighting off all the luns they could without themselves going under. The river was fast and relentless, and dangerously overcrowded.

The luns that were still running along the bank almost immediately drew their longbows and prepared to fire from the riverbanks.

"Don't let them shoot!" Levi's voice commanded through the chaos. Several flens shot back with their own bows, buying them enough time to get out of reach of their pursuers.

The river was still a dangerous horse to ride, and Nigeb constantly found himself being dragged back onto the tree trunk by Athor, who wielded his sword in one hand and constantly steadied his companion with the other, using only his thighs to stay seated himself.

The current quickly carried the flens off, leaving their pursuers behind. The jungle rushed by, and mountains began looming up on either side. They were now coming into a large valley.

Nigeb had remembered seeing this valley on the Map of Azoons. It was the valley in which the Temple of Truth was located, and only now did the young flen remember seeing on the map the river which flowed from one end of the island to the other.

This was the river that would lead them to where the temple was located.

The other flens had evidently figured that out, for they began pushing toward the far bank, the one on which the Temple of Truth was to be and also where the luns wouldn't be. They soon managed to stop their movement and climb out of the river and ascend the bank, although it took them considerable time to all find each other.

There was no doubt that the luns wouldn't be far behind, and the flens set to scouring the valley.

The valley itself, located around the middle of the island, was surrounded on all sides by mountains, which loomed high in the air. The valley floor was stony and full of hills, with the occasional flatland on which grass grew. Overall, it was very different from the dense jungles and tropical air which the flens had just been in.

"We must find the temple before nightfall," Levi called out. "Otherwise we shall be overtaken by the luns, and will no longer have the light by which to search."

"Then we have little time," Athor replied. "For sunset will reach us soon, and the luns sooner."

They spread out as they searched the valley, looking for any sign of the presence of a large structure, and staying within hearing distance. Already the sun began descending down, so that they had little more than an hour's worth of time, and the relentless pursuit of the luns began to draw nearer. The flens could hear yelling on the other end of the river, and the stomping of feet.

One could imagine the frightful situation that the company found themselves in. They were now ascending the opposite end of the valley. They couldn't go back; their only hope was to find the Temple of Truth. What happened then could only be guessed.

Flens can run far and fast at the same time, building up to speeds that men do not know of. When forced to run day and night on end, they can do so tremendously, outlasting by far any other running creature. Many running arts and achievements can be credited to them, and they are always willing to display their talent.

The flens did admirably well in staying far ahead of their pursuers, but the day had had its affects on them, and soon they began to tire at a frightful speed, like one who has nothing left in him.

As Nigeb leaped up the steep slope, feeling the last of his strength failing him, he looked up and gave a startled cry.

Far above him, protruding from the very mountainside itself, was a large structure with two enormous columns and a door at the center, carved out of the rock alone. A stairway led down from it for nearly a hundred feet, blending into the surrounding landscape.

Nigeb's cry brought the other flens running as fast as their tired feet could carry them. Most saw the temple before they even reached Nigeb, due to his wild pointing and yelling, and all eight of them speedily ascended the stairway.

Flens are quick and light-footed, so that even in their pitiable state they reached the doorway with astonishing speed.

Athor grabbed the large brass handle and pulled the door back.

But it remained firmly shut.

Chapter 13

The Temple of Truth

"HELP HIM!" LEVI COMMANDED, and grasped part of the handle. Several other flens did so too, and pulled with all that was in them, but to no avail.

The outer part of the temple, the part that was visible to the flens, was a dull gray color, the same as the rock it was cut out of. The columns stood at the height of nearly thirty feet, until they cut into the very cliffside itself. The door, which the flens were so desperately pulling, was about twelve feet tall, and six feet wide, with the large brass handle, about one foot in diameter, attached to the lefthand side. Otherwise, there were very few characteristics of the Temple of Truth on the outside.

Nearly all of the flens were now pulling on the handle, grunting and grumbling, more out of fear than anger.

Now that they had stopped running, the luns drew ever nearer, and their shapes could be made out as they crossed the valley floor. They would be there in less than a quarter of an hour.

Nigeb sat down on the ground, cross-legged, and peered intently at the cliffside from under his eyebrows.

The flens were now pushing on the door with everything they had, and had even begun beating it with their tools and weapons, in hope of bringing it down by force. Nigeb knew that there had to be some other way. There was no keyhole, and it wouldn't open by force, either.

How he wished that Eranor was there! Surely, he would know how to act. And yet, Nigeb now knew the full weight of becoming an Azoon. He knew that somewhere, somehow, Eranor was watching over them and working all things out, but much depended on the flens themselves, and their friendship with the son of Dominum was a two-way thing.

They could not give up! Not now that they had gone so far! But despair was nearly upon them.

"Quick, give me the map!" Levi said, and then looked intently at it. But no clue could be found as to how they were to open the door.

"If there is no way in naturally," Nigeb said, "then there must be a password, or some other such trick."

"But what?" Levi asked. He then turned to face the door, and began mumbling different words in Flenish. He tried *open* and *enter,* and went as far as saying several different names of importance from the days of Old.

"Wait," Oser said, after the door remained steadfast. "If a seeker of the Temple of Truth were to come and attempt to pronounce the password, but didn't speak Flenish, how would he enter, providing that the password was in our language? This is the Temple of Truth, not treachery. It must be simple."

"If it is the Temple of Truth that we seek, then it is truth itself which we seek." Levi said. Then he commanded, "Help."

As he said so, there was a shake in the ground, as if an earthquake had made up its mind to begin its shaking, and then had suddenly left. The door swung smoothly open, revealing a long, dark passage, the end of which was not seen.

The passage was approximately the same height and width as the door, with smooth, polished walls. Into it the flens plunged without a second thought. Nigeb, at the end of the line, turned around in time to see the luns ascending the slope. Without further ado, he heaved the monstrous door shut with a finalizing thud.

A great deal of commotion went up as the flens suddenly found themselves in complete darkness. Shouting and yelling instantly went to full volume, with lots of tripping and growling. The sudden fright that they experienced, on top of what had already happened that day, was enough to cause chaos for several long moments, before the flens succeeded in lighting a match.

After getting a bearing of their surroundings, they organized themselves, managed to light more torches, and began descending down the tunnel, their only current option.

As they began trudging along, Nigeb, at the rear (again), seemed to hear a soft patter and thudding from the other side of the door. The luns, he assumed, had reached the door, only to find their prey escaped, and their way barred. The door was extraordinarily thick and resolute, so that all their efforts sounded pathetic.

The air in the tunnel was fresh, but the farther they went, the more dense and unnatural it became. The stone floor absorbed the sound of their footsteps, so that the eerie quiet was only disturbed by their breathing.

As the tunnel came to an end, it opened up into a vast cavern of a most extraordinary network of tunnels and roadways, all carved of stone and rock, but elaborately constructed and built. The unimaginable architecture of civilizations long forgotten was to be found in this hall of breathtaking awe, the desire of flens' hearts.

The ceiling stretched far above their heads, supported by enormous columns. The flens became overwhelmed with wonder and the understanding of how remarkably small they were.

But among the immensely huge and inconceivable wonder and mystery of the world that we often find ourselves in, there lurks a vast darkness, unchallenged, older than the stars, more hideous than any creature in existence, at the core of all that is evil and ill-intentioned. It was behind every corner, in every dark place, it had its relentless grip on the world and all who wished death and darkness. Nigeb felt it first, the mind-consuming desire to give up. His limbs began trembling, his eyes darted to and fro, and he resisted the impulse to scream of utter horror.

It was that old enemy of the world and of Dominum. The flens all felt it to their very bones, even before the shadow appeared and began to grow.

The shadow, which had now consumed nearly a quarter of the cavern, morphed and changed, until before the flens there came into perception a most hideous and evil dragon, black in color, and as big as an elephant, with claws as swords, and teeth as spears.

Nigeb could not look into those fiery, hateful eyes which the beast possessed.

The flens shuddered and faltered as the dragon prowled round them, keeping a distance, so that they could not get a full view of it, for the shadows grew as it neared and completely covered the thing at times.

"So," it growled in its most menacing and dreadful voice, "eight flens, chosen by Dominum's son, have come to the Temple of Truth. You have come to learn the secret of the Armor of Light, have you not? But what you have not foreseen is the wretched end of your little company, have you not, as all good things must certainly end?"

Levi stepped forward in the direction of the dragon. "You lie," he said. Then he spoke in Flenish. "Gil-Galude!" *The Hondaloom.*

"Do I?" the Hondaloom answered, as he continued his prowling. "You are mere mortals, incapable of resisting me, born of the world, and therefore belonging to the king of it. Me! You cannot see what I see, you cannot go where I go. Your doom is near; it is inevitable."

His invisible hand and deceitful words were weaving in between the company, searching for a weakness, some means to get the best of them.

But the flens stood strong still.

Levi answered. "Hope is perhaps the best of all things. It strengthens the weak, it supports the failing of heart, and hope never ends. But greater still, we now know the giver of hope, so that our hope is not empty. And that giver of hope is the true King of Erandin!"

The Hondaloom gnashed his teeth, and slunk into the shadows, but only for a moment. He then reappeared round the next corner and continued. "How can you know the way of things? You have not the knowledge of the all-powerful strength of Dominum, nor do you know the power of the enemy you go against. How can you stand against the onslaught of evil? What if Dominum will stand beside you not?"

Levi replied to this. "Dominum created Erandin to be rightful King over it. Surely he will return it to its former glory, and rid it of evil, as it once was? We have this hope."

"What is your testimony, then, O flen of such courage?" the Hondaloom nearly barked.

To this Levi replied as follows:

I saw the one with the power unending in his hand, as I went one day along the dunes and the sand.
Without him the sun shone not, and the moon ceased its rise. I saw the world, past and future, as I looked into his eyes.
I left the ground and walked among the stars, and saw a reality known not to men.
It took me a while to come back into my own, and when I had done so, he said, "come out of the darkness and into the light!"

"I see that I have made a mistake in asking you first, young flen of such a testimony," the Hondaloom growled. "But I doubt that the others could confirm to their own such testimony?"

"Wrong again, Gil-Galude!" Oser replied. "I myself have such a testimony! It is the testimony of all who truly meet Eranor. The jewels and gold of this world dimmed and my death became not in vain, when I gained the free friendship of him who saw Erandin come into existence! When I learned that he was coming back to claim this land as rightful King, my life became to tell of him and his power!"

"All of us have met with him!" Tenzin said readily. "You have not succeeded in stopping us, and you cannot now!"

"We shall see, for you do not know everything!" the Hondaloom replied. "For you to reach Dominum's land, you must first cross the Great Chasm. And who can jump the Great Chasm? Who can build a bridge that would stretch from one end to the other? Who can descend into its depths and come out on the other side? No one can!"

And with that, the evil Hondaloom shot out of the darkness, barreling towards the company with great intensity and power. As he did so, his jaws opened to release a monstrous bolt of flame, which split through the group's core as the flens leapt aside, half in one direction, half in the other.

Chapter 14

The Last Stand

NIGEB STUMBLED AND THREW himself down a passage, scraping his knees on the stone stairs and busting his chin. He had lost his bearings and was not aware of what had happened to his friends. Searing heat engulfed him and flames licked at his boots, but the damp, dark passage obscured him from damage.

He became aware of someone tumbling onto him.

Thon rolled over, kicking at the smoldering ashes on his clothes. Most of the fire had died out almost as quickly as it had started, due to there not being any burnable objects in the Temple of Truth, but the flens had nearly been roasted in the process.

Nigeb wiped the soot from his face and began crawling farther down the passage. As he did so, Firm burst into the passage with Athor right behind him.

In a display of strength, Athor hauled both Nigeb *and* Thon to their feet, and then began dragging them up a flight of stairs, with Firm bringing up the rear.

"Get to the high ground!" Athor shouted.

"Where are the others?" Nigeb gasped.

"Unhurt, if that's what you mean," Athor answered. "They retreated down to the entrance that we came in by."

"Why are we going up?!" Thon asked. "The Hondaloom is a dragon, and dragons can fly!"

"The Hondaloom disappeared, and we're not sure where he went. It's the luns that are the problem. They are coming."

Almost on cue, a loud, rhythmic drumbeating reached their ears, a frightening *boom, boom, boom.*

The speed of the flens doubled. Nobody had to convince them of the danger they were in.

They had come to the Temple of Truth seeking the Armor of Light, but had unexpectedly encountered the Hondaloom, and now his luns had infiltrated the temple. The flens had not learned the secret to the Armor of Light, and Eranor was not there either. There was no safety there.

The flens fled up the stairway, down a wide passage, and then up a stairway again.

"How did the luns enter?" Thon asked, his voice a little shaky.

"That is out of our knowledge," Athor replied. "But most possibly it was the Hondaloom's doing. He might have brought the door down."

Athor suddenly turned down a passage that didn't lead up, but that led above where the fire had been, towards the front entrance of the temple.

"Where are we going?" Thon asked.

"Prepare your swords!" Athor announced. "We shall not leave our friends in danger! For Eranor!"

Athor raced down the passage, disappearing around a corner. Thon and Firm drew their own swords and raced after him. Nigeb pulled out his sword, nearly dropped it, fixed his grip, and then followed.

The passage turned and then led a considerable distance, taking them all the way back to where they had entered, but not quite to the front door. As with everywhere in the Temple of Truth, the bare surfaces of the passage were a dull, smooth gray, being occasionally beautifully painted or covered in gold.

The flens could now hear a clear banging and thumping, as if an elephant was passing by.

Nigeb entered an arched doorway and found himself in a large, dark room with several columns and doorways. They had found the other four flens, who had drawn their swords and were fully armed. Nigeb and the other three joined them as they positioned themselves in a tactical battle position, all facing a large double-door. Behind this door could be heard the pounding and shuffling of a large number of armed warriors.

"Do not let them pass through," Levi said. "This is the only chance we have of stopping them."

Nigeb, who had stationed himself at the end of the group, looked around. All the doors except the one that they had entered by were bolted shut. There was only one way to escape. And it didn't lead out of the temple.

The flens were outnumbered and trapped. They did not have the secret of the Armor of Light, and the Hondaloom was close by. There were very few things that could save them now. And Eranor was nowhere to be seen. The situation was getting steadily worse.

A loud booming sound came from behind the door, as the luns battered away at it. The door groaned and bounced on its hinges, but refused to open.

The flens stacked up piles of debris against the door, piling wood and stones to keep it from opening.

But the luns began hacking away at the door using their swords and axes, forcing their weapons through and slowly breaking it apart.

The door finally burst open with terrific force, throwing back the flens as several dozen luns rushed in.

The flens had arranged themselves in a triangle, ensuring that the luns would not be able to pass easily. As Levi had said earlier, they could on no account allow the luns to pass through, or else they would surely lose the fight. They absolutely had to stop them there and then.

As the luns surged forward, the flens pushed back, desperately fighting for ground. This was the third time they faced off against the luns of the Hondaloom, and this was to be the greatest battle of the three.

Nigeb's sword flared with his name as several luns collapsed on him. He parried the blows of two luns and forced them back while using his shield to protect himself from the others. But he was immediately pushed back with sheer strength as the luns hacked at his shield.

He was slammed against a wall as he fought back, slipping and stumbling. He hacked at a lun's leg, causing that lun to fall, and aimed a blow at another lun using the edge of his shield.

But he was a long way from winning.

As four swords were pointed at him from four different directions, he leaped desperately away. Indeed, he had so little space to work with that his shoulder brushed against the surface of the wall as he leaped past the luns.

Kevin and Tenzin had fastened their bows and were covering the rest of the flens from the ever-present shooting of the luns. Levi and Athor were battling the bodyguard of Yar, with Oser right behind them.

Nigeb scrambled away from the luns in hot pursuit of him, right as Thon and Firm came to his rescue, and the tables were turned.

The luns were quickly beaten back by the three flens.

Not just that, but shouts rang out where the battle had been raging in its hottest, and Nigeb looked up to see the bodyguard fleeing in all directions, with Levi and Athor advancing on Yar and his remaining luns, who quickly scattered in all directions. All retreated through the door that they had come in.

But as the last of the luns fled, something far more sinister entered that battle-worn room.

It wasn't mortal or made of flesh. It was a shadow. A dark figure of evil. Something that screamed in the resemblance of the Hondaloom. Something ancient and imperishable.

The flens saw a figure clad in shapeless black, with no face and no heart. But its presence spoke far more than its appearance. This was a Dark Ghost.

As it rushed at them with its fiery sword drawn, the room was suddenly filled with darkness.

Chapter 15

Lies and Half-Truths

FIRM WAS SUDDENLY AWARE of something like a strong undercurrent dragging him away in the darkness. He tumbled several times, trying to free himself, but he was held in a deathlike grip. He managed to yell right before he felt himself lost from the presence of the other flens.

When he finally tumbled out into the light, he found himself in a dimly lit room, with various objects lying on the floor, such as books and tools. The room was shaped like a cube, with no openings save a large door at the end. Firm tried to force his way out, but found it barred shut, most probably from the outside. In the center of the room was a large block, carved from stone. On this block Firm was forced to sit and think.

He was beginning to become frightfully scared. The adventure to Flenvinhum was far more than it seemed on the surface. Something deep and powerful was involved. Eranor was at the midst of it. It was all just beginning.

But now Firm was lost. He had absolutely no idea of where he was, and was dreadfully uncertain of what was to come next.

Was he going to just be stuck here? Surely Eranor or his friends would save him?

Out of sheer desperation, Firm yelled out, "Where am I?"

What a frightful thing it was to find out that he was not, after all, all alone. Out of the darkness came a voice sounding like Eranor's, but, alas, with an edge of malice. Firm knew right away who it was.

"You are lost," the voice answered.

"I know you are there, Gil-Galude!" Firm shouted.

"But you do not know where exactly," the Hondaloom answered. "So how can you fight me?"

Firm pulled out his sword with a zing. He had not lost it.

"Ah, you pull out your sword, I see," the voice came. "How pathetic! You are unworthy of it! You have failed it already!"

"You are a liar!" Firm yelled into the darkness.

"Am I?" the Hondaloom answered. "If I am not mistaken, you have already lost it once! Think back to when you fought the luns on your sailboat. When you were taken, you lost your sword! You had it not with you! Your friends had to bring it along and give it to you! See? You are unworthy of it, and you will lose it again soon."

Firm did not want to believe this, but his mind raced back to those few moments when he was taken and then freed, and to when Levi had first given him his sword, telling him to keep it with honor.

The Hondaloom continued. "You are a failure! Eranor was wrong when he chose you! You do not see it, but I do. Even now your friends are wondering how you could have possibly gotten lost again.

"You cannot match up to your fellow flens and you mustn't even try. At the South Bridge you did nothing but flee. As your company fought, you lingered behind to save your own skin. You were too afraid to even try. Likewise, at sea you couldn't even put up a fight. You were taken captive right away, as the other flens fought for their lives. Am I not telling the truth?"

"How do you know all that?" Firm shouted out, still not sure of where to shout exactly.

"I am everywhere and I see everything," the Hondaloom responded. Then he continued.

"You do not fit in, and you have been a burden to them all along. You cannot fight, you have no survival skills, you are not resourceful, and you understand nothing of good and evil. You look to Eranor for help, but even there you fail. Eranor cannot help nor does he want to: he is the son of Dominum, he was present when Erandin was created, so why would he care about you?

"Moreover, you are stuck in Erandin, where I am king and where I rule freely. You cannot jump the Great Chasm; you cannot reach Dominum's land."

Firm wanted to shout out a defiant reply, but he was beginning to despair. The Hondaloom had truthfully listed Firm's failures and shortcomings, and the young flen was now beginning to believe everything that his enemy said. The Hondaloom's voice was sounding more and more like Eranor's, and Firm shrank under every blow. His sword was slipping out of his hand. The darkness began to consume him. He could see a gigantic sword slowly coming towards him.

But as depressing, deathlike thoughts ran through his head, something came back to him. An idea. A remembrance.

Firm shouted out. "Hondaloom, we, as dwellers of Erandin, according to Eranor, have a choice of whether or not we shall become Azoons under Dominum. As someone who had made the choice of becoming an Azoon from the beginning by committing myself to finding the Temple of Truth, I hereby call upon the name of Eranor to my aid against my enemies!"

Nothing happened. Everything came to a sudden halt as the stillness overtook the conversation. The darkness became darker. Firm felt the shadows around him increasing.

Then the Hondaloom began to laugh.

It was a spiteful, evil laugh, that resonated throughout the rooms and halls of the Temple of Truth, growing louder every moment. Finally, the Hondaloom spoke.

"Where is Eranor? I see him not!"

But as the Hondaloom gloated, a figure rose up onto the stone in the center of the room. It cast back its cloak, and Eranor came forth in all his shining glory. He was wearing a white, fiery armor with a blazing white sword in one hand and a radiating shield in the other. It was indeed the Armor of Light. It cleaved back the darkness and the shadows shrank.

"You are wrong, Hondaloom!" Eranor cried out. "I have been here since the beginning of your conversation! I have heard your lies, and now I come to intervene and protect my own."

"You cannot protect your flens!" the Hondaloom hissed.

"I can if they will follow me." Eranor replied. "Now, begone! Go back into the shadows. You have no power over me as you do over Erandin! By the power of Dominum, I banish you!"

"You cannot do so!" the Hondaloom shrieked, but there was a note of emptiness in his threats.

"I am on Dominum's behalf in Erandin, and I banish you! Begone!"

With a final piercing shriek, the Hondaloom vanished, taking the darkness away with him. The room brightened and took on a more cheery air. The Armor of Light faded away and was gone.

Now only Eranor and Firm remained, the latter breathing deeply. Finally, Firm asked. "How did you banish him?"

"My father has power over everything in his land and in Erandin," Eranor replied. "Nothing exists or happens without him. He holds all that he created in his hands. He is the beginning and the end. Even evil forces fear him and are helpless before him. But Erandin has chosen to turn against him and rely on itself. It is all a choice, you see, and everyone has it, the choice to side with Dominum or with the Hondaloom. Those who choose against Dominum only lose themselves all the more."

"Will I be able to do what you did?" Firm asked, quietly.

"Not yet," Eranor answered. "The Hondaloom still rules Erandin and all that are bound to it. But soon, very soon, I hope that you will have the power and freedom to do so. Great things are in store. Let us now come to the aid of your friends."

Chapter 16

The Awakening

NIGEB FELT HIMSELF BEING rushed away in a current of darkness.

And then he hit the ground.

His first thought was how cold it was. But very quickly he began to feel that terror, that same evil lurking in the darkness, the same helplessness. He knew that something was near, but he knew not where.

He was unaware of his surroundings, and as he staggered up in the darkness, he felt his way around. But all he felt was the smooth surface of the floor and the walls. It was as if his eyes were not open.

And how many walls there were! Cold, unmoving walls that could be hiding anything behind the next corner.

He began moving, unable to see, or, at best, just catching glimpses of shapes in the darkness. He went with one hand on a wall, hoping to better navigate this way.

But then he ran into a wall, nearly screaming in the process, so nervous he was. It was perhaps a good thing that he kept quiet and did not disturb the stillness.

He corrected his position, and began following the new wall.

But within a few steps he ran into another wall, this one catching him completely unaware. He fell flat on the ground.

When he got up, he followed that same wall until he came to an opening that he was able to pass through. He then ran into yet another wall.

It was clear to him now that he was in a maze.

Surely he was still in the Temple of Truth. But even then he couldn't be certain.

He still remembered all that had happened concerning the Hondaloom, the luns, and that dreadful figure that he had seen. Where his friends were now he could only guess.

As he sat against the wall, planning to weep in frustration, he felt his sword, still buckled around his waist. The same sword that held such a history. First it belonged to his father, carried through so many adventures that Nigeb could only guess of. Then, falling into unworthy hands, it was carried by Yar until recovered back by Nigeb, in a most extraordinary way, so that there could be no doubt that it was Eranor who recovered it. And through the map that it carried, the flens were now here, on the island of SafeHaven, in the Temple of Truth, here to find the Armor of Light.

Nigeb forced himself up. What a history he was to have. He was ready. Drawing his sword, his name flashed across the blade, momentarily lighting up Nigeb's surroundings.

As it did so, Nigeb caught sight of a tunnel, leading as far as the eye could see. It slanted downward, but was fairly large around. Down this tunnel Nigeb went.

His sword stayed dimly lit, but otherwise he could see little at all.

He stumbled and nearly fell, but encountered no walls. However, as he went along, he began hearing almost a rustling sound from behind him, farther up the tunnel. It was as if someone who didn't quite walk was very quietly following him.

Nigeb spun around and slowly ran back up the tunnel, his sword flashing. He fancied he caught a glimpse of a shadow retreating up the tunnel. As he froze, looking intently around, he thought he heard more rustling farther down the tunnel.

He turned around and slowly began descending, warily looking behind his back, and pausing every once in a while. But all he could hear was his own heartbeat and heavy breathing. And though he was alone, he could feel an encounter approaching.

A shadow suddenly appeared ahead of him, advancing at full speed. Nigeb was faintly aware of a second shadow, approaching from the back. As he readied himself, he was slammed from the side as a third shadow leaped from the wall.

He crashed against the tunnel wall as a metallic shriek pierced the silence and filled him with terror.

Nigeb swung his sword and stabbed at the shadow, but his weapon seemingly went through the figure and left it unharmed. The young flen suddenly remembered what Eranor had said about the Hondaloom being a spirit, and not having flesh and bones. He also remembered his encounter with the four luns in the forest. They had thought him to be a Dark Ghost. What faced him were also Dark Ghosts, and they weren't mortal, either.

Nigeb parried several blows and tried unsuccessfully to penetrate his opponent, but as another scream pierced the air, he fell over and dropped his sword.

As the shadows attacked him from the top, he remembered one more thing.

It was from back when he had first met Eranor at the Monastery, when Dominum's son had spoken to him about his parents.

There was a key in his words, something dearly important.

Eranor had said that Nigeb would be under his protection.

Nigeb had only one thing to do.

"Help! I call upon the protection of Eranor, the son of Dominum!" he yelled with all that was in his lungs.

The Dark Ghosts froze for a moment, as if stunned.

Then there was a flash of light as Eranor stood up in their midst, wearing the Armor of Light.

The Dark Ghosts shrank away, and fell at his first blow. They disappeared before Nigeb's very eyes, as did the overwhelming terror.

Eranor reached out his hand and clasped Nigeb's, handing the flen's fallen sword with the other.

"Follow me!" he commanded as he began ascending the tunnel Nigeb had just gone down. The young flen quickly realized what a mistake he had made.

The young flen ran with all that he had, but would never have kept up with Eranor had not some unexplainable force seemingly pulled him forward, keeping him alongside Dominum's son. The two flew down tunnels and around corners, passing through a hopelessly unending maze, until Eranor pulled him from the darkness and into the light.

Even as Nigeb stepped out, he saw with joy all seven of his fellow flens, unharmed (mostly), but wearily keeping guard, and readying themselves for another encounter.

The flens shouted and cheered, happy at the reunion, but turned to Eranor, rather hopelessly.

"You are here now, Eranor," Levi said. "Surely you can defeat these things of horror and rid us of this place."

"You shall get your rest soon enough, my dear flens," Eranor answered. "But for now, this fight isn't over. You must learn to use the Armor of Light. I shall protect you from what you cannot defend yourselves against, but you must become a part of this battle against the evil of the Hondaloom. You must call upon the Armor of Light, as you have called upon me."

Even as he spoke, shadows began entering the large, bare room that they were in. Dark Ghosts, a dozen at least, began slowly drifting in, and the room became darker and filled with the essence of fear. As these dreadful things advanced, the flens continued to look at Eranor.

Eranor smiled. "You are now Azoons. You already have the key to the Armor of Light."

The room steadily became darker than the night, and all was quiet yet.

But just as those dreadful Dark Ghosts began to close in, brandishing their long red swords, which burned with hatred and evil, Firm, it seemed, understood something.

What it was he understood I cannot fully say, but I know that the room lit up with the fiery presence of the Armor of Light as the darkness was thrown back and the Dark Ghosts faltered even as they lifted their weapons.

Firm was wearing the Armor of Light, fully clad with a complete set of armor and a helmet, wielding a bright sword and shield, just as Eranor had moments before. Light radiated from every part of his armor and he sprang at the Dark Ghosts with renewed strength and courage.

And just like that, Nigeb found the key and obtained the Armor of Light. Levi did likewise, and Thon, along with Athor, Oser, Kevin, and Tenzin.

The eight Azoons met the Dark Ghosts in heated battle.

The servants of the Hondaloom no longer had the advantage of surprise and darkness. Light flashed from the Azoons' armor, and they advanced with a fighting spirit that they never knew they had.

The horror and terror that the Dark Ghosts possessed were worthless against the bravery of the Azoons, their weapons could not pierce the Armor of Light, and the Azoons cleaved them down with swords that burned with fiery anger against these servants of the Hondaloom.

The Azoons stood unmoving, like a stone wall, blocking out the darkness and withstanding the ferocity of their enemies. The Dark Ghosts rushed upon the young Azoons, and were beaten back immediately, stricken at from left and right, pierced with the light. They rushed again and again, countless times, but the young flens could not be defeated.

One by one the Dark Ghosts fell, blown into oblivion by the swords of the Armor of Light. Their numbers dwindled down, becoming dangerously low, until the Azoons rushed the three that were left.

Levi reached them first, bringing down his sword in a high arc that smote the first Dark Ghost, shattering his wicked sword and cleaving him in half. The dark shape faded away to nothing.

The second one sprang at Kevin and Oser, intent on ending both their lives. But its sword rang off the armor with a *clang* as it sought to impale Kevin's heart, and the young flen responded with his own blow, this one far more deadly. As the Dark Ghost flailed, Oser ended it with a final blow.

The last one threw its sword in a spiral at them in a last effort to end them, before turning and fleeing. The sword sailed through the air in a display of red before colliding with several of the Azoons, and knocking most of them to the ground, though not penetrating their armor.

But as the Dark Ghost fled the room, Athor pursued it, and caught it at the door, where he ended it with his sword.

After that, with the battle won, all was quiet and still.

Then Eranor, who had been quietly leaning on his staff and watching from the exit of the maze, spoke up.

Chapter 17

The Last Chapter

"Now you know the secret to the Armor of Light," Eranor said. "You have been given a gift against the Hondaloom and his servants, the Dark Ghosts. But this gift is for withstanding this deep evil, not what is less dark. Beware of using it unwisely. It is a gift you receive from my father, Dominum. He may give it, and he may take it away. But all those who are true of heart and purpose will not be disappointed by it."

Levi came forward and knelt before Eranor. When he looked up he said. "What must happen now?"

Eranor struck the floor with the bottom end of his staff. Then he offered his hand to Levi and helped him rise.

"It has already begun and will not end until the very end. My dear flens, you have persevered through much today, but it is not over until the Hondaloom is defeated and you are free to go to my father's land. But that is my battle. You would never defeat the Hondaloom on your own, and that is why I have come. But you have become part of my battle, and it is long from over. Come now, let us leave for home, and then we can rest."

It was only then that the flens remembered exactly where they were, which was deep in the Temple of Truth, far into the untamed island of SafeHaven, off the coast of Erandin. They remembered the Monastery back in Flenvinhum, the comforts and security it provided, and the fact that it was all far away from evil . . .

The eight flens, now Azoons, left the Temple of Truth, accompanied by Eranor. Sooner or later they found their way out and onto the landscape of the valley, where the sun was just beginning to rise over the horizon.

The flens really had lost track of time in the temple. They had, after all, entered the previous evening, and had spent an entire night there, hardly realizing it.

All day the flens trekked through the jungles and hot climate of SafeHaven, up and down hills, through the valley and around mountains, as best as they could. They encountered the river that they had used for escape earlier, and followed it back to shore. There, they found that there were no luns at all, that the camp had been taken down, and that the luns had left in their ship.

Very soon the flens found their own ship, as well as the rowboat. Soon they set sail for the coast of Erandin.

No storms troubled them and neither did the luns. They arrived a day later at the coast of Erandin, and then traveled swiftly through the lands until they once again reached Flenvinhum, as they had three weeks earlier.

When they finally made it to the Monastery, it was decided that Nigeb, Thon, and Firm were to return to Ullantown for a few weeks' time to see their families once more before returning back to the Monastery.

It would be a long journey, longer than the first time, as the three flens would be going around most of the lands and places they had passed earlier, in order to avoid trouble and danger, but they all agreed that it would be worth it to be home again.

But before they left, Nigeb had one question to ask of Levi, who was staying with the other four flens and Eranor.

"I was lost in that maze and was attacked by the Dark Ghosts, but, tell me, what became of the rest of you? Where did those things take you seven?"

Levi smiled grimly, thinking about his own experience.

"I believe all of us, not just you and me, were taken to that maze, where the Dark Ghosts intended to end us but where each one of us was saved by Eranor when we called upon his name. I know I was. However, I believe that Firm was tested separately by the Hondaloom, until he too called upon the name of Eranor. But I do not know the entire story, and I doubt we need to.

"Go now to your homeland, my friend. See your family, tell them that all is well, but be prepared. Evil war hosts come from the East. There will be conflict yet."

The three flens returned to Ullantown, following the coastline and arriving six weeks later. They could vaguely see the outline of the White Mountain as they passed it. They made sure to stay as far away as possible from the forest of Wolf's Fear and the first forest as well, but caught sight of the canyon over which the South Bridge stretched, many miles away. They encountered no luns, but took several precautions in order to avoid any risks, there being only three of them on three horses and armed only with their swords, the Armor of Light being something they wouldn't use against enemies made of flesh and bones.

Finally, as the flens rode over a hill and caught sight of Ullantown for the first time in months, Nigeb felt a wave of contentment and happiness, and a feeling of excitement to be home at last.

But the face of Eranor came into his mind's eye, and Nigeb knew that it was the friendship of Dominum's son that propelled him forward to whatever destiny he was to have.

Nigeb had not retired.